T0146445

A CARNIVAL IN
MY HEART AND
OTHER STORIES

Books by Kenneth C. Gardner, Jr.

Novels
The Song Is Ended (2011)
The Dark Between The Stars (2012)
Travels On The Road To America (2015)

Collections
Meatball Birds and Seven Other Stories (2013)
"And All Our Yesterdays..." and Nine Other Stories (2014)
Maggie: A Girl and Nine Other Stories (2016)

Non-Fiction
Echoes of Distant School Bells: A History of the Drayton Public School, 1879-1998, Volume 1 (1994); Volume 2 (1999)

A CARNIVAL IN MY HEART AND OTHER STORIES

KENNETH C. GARDNER, JR.

 iUniverse

A CARNIVAL IN MY HEART AND OTHER STORIES

iUniverse books may be ordered through booksellers or by contacting:

iUniverse
1663 Liberty Drive
Bloomington, IN 47403
www.iuniverse.com
1-800-Authors (1-800-288-4677)

ISBN: 978-1-5320-3458-9 (sc)
ISBN: 978-1-5320-3459-6 (e)

Print information available on the last page.

iUniverse rev. date: 10/20/2017

For grandparents everywhere who know…
"Tho' much is taken, much abides; and tho'
We are not now that strength which in old days
Moved earth and heaven; that which we are, we are;
One equal temper of heroic hearts,
Made weak by time and fate, but strong in will
To strive, to seek, to find, and not to yield."
Tennyson, "Ulysses"

CONTENTS

MY ANGEL..1
CAPTAIN MIDNIGHT AND THE TOM MIX RALSTON
STRAIGHT SHOOTER 13
UNDER THE SIGN OF AQUARIUS 29
MAGGIE: A FINAL CHAPTER 43
A CARNIVAL IN MY HEART 53
DOCTOR BEDARD MEETS THE CHURCHES...........87
"ALL THAT GLITTERS…" 97
GOD WILL PROVIDE 113
C. EDGAR BUCKMAN 123
IT'S A GRAND OLD FLAG 129
THE ISLAND 139
"HELLO, MY NAME IS LYDIA LEE" 149
THE OLD MAN 165
A LOVE STORY 171
A SAGA..185

CONTENTS

MY ANGEL

Alv Andreassen could make anything out of metal or stone, if he was sober. He had the equipment in his blacksmith shop on Villard West in Menninger, North Dakota, to work with iron, steel, tin, marble, granite, cement, just about any material if he had stayed away from the bottle. He had done excellent forge welding, but with the coming of acetylene, his welding took on an even better success rate.

Because of his talent, Alv was popular with the men of the area. If he was in the mood and someone showed up with work for him, he'd bring out some liquor and raise a toast with the customer on the new venture.

Alv was not popular with the ladies, however. For one thing, he used curse words in his everyday conversation, even if a woman happened to be present, although in that case some of the more corrosive words didn't come out. But more importantly, he didn't treat his wife Kristina very well. Tina, as she was known, seemed about half the size of Alv, who stood a few inches over six feet and weighed at least 250 lbs. She had come off the farm to work in the kitchen and dining room of the Hotel Woodson on St. Paul, but was so shy she was always in danger of losing her job as a waitress for not being more friendly with the customers.

When Alv got the job of putting in cement sidewalks along St. Paul, he stopped in at the Woodson for supper and that was when he met Tina. Soon he was eating there all the time, and eventually they

1

were seen on buggy rides, and she even got him into the Norwegian Lutheran Church on Lamborn, a building he'd never entered before.

Alv had a small house next to his business, and that's where they were married, with just her family, two witnesses, and the preacher in attendance. Her mother and sisters took a long time to forgive her for not asking them to help with the preparations. Alv's family had remained in Norway.

Mr. Woodson gave them a wedding supper or else there wouldn't have been one.

The wedding night was spent in the little house. The next morning Alv went to work and was not in a good mood. Tina stayed indoors for two days before venturing uptown for groceries. No one could imagine what she did for two days; the house wasn't that big that it needed much cleaning.

She never talked about that night, not even with her mother or sisters, but there never were any children.

Alv's business grew, but so did his bills. He had hired men to work for him and took on more jobs, but staying solvent was a near-run thing, and he almost lost his shop to creditors. Then Tina stepped in and took over the bookkeeping. Within a year the business was safe. Alv began calling Tina "My Angel."

As he became more prosperous, Alv began drinking more. North Dakota had come into the Union in 1889 as a "dry" state, but Alv had no trouble buying booze from the many blind pigs around town.

Soon his business was hitting rocky financial shoals again. Tina stepped in, sold off his cement division, which reduced his payroll, and she was "My Angel" once more.

Tina was a member of the Ladies' Aid, and although she was elected as an officer from time to time, she did most of her work behind the scenes. The town may not have realized the hours she spent preparing food baskets for the poor or getting everything just so for the annual church bazaar, but the other members of the Ladies' Aid knew, so when Mrs. Stanford, who lived across the alley from Alv and Tina, heard the abuse he hurled at her and duly reported it to her friends, the female animosity toward Alv increased.

At least he never beat or struck her. She never had bruises or broken bones like some wives had.

One of the most abused wives had been Ethelene MacGregor. Her husband Robert, better known as "Mac," used her like a punching bag, but always behind closed doors. When she would go to the doctor with a fractured wrist or finger or a broken eardrum, she always had a story about some accident that was her fault.

Even so, gossip spread among the women who were afraid Ethelene would be killed. They began putting pressure on their husbands, fathers, and brothers to do something to save Ethelene, but the men needed some form of proof that Mac was the culprit the women painted him to be.

One evening the MacGregors were walking down Villard next to Davenport's Department Store, a brick building that stretched from Chicago Street to the alley. They were arguing about something. Art Holder was in the alley between Davenport's and the bank when he heard the angry voices. He peered around the corner of Davenport's just in time to see Mac look up and down Villard and then smack his wife on the side of her head, knocking her to the cement.

Just as she was hitting the sidewalk, Mr. and Mrs. Seth Marsh came around the other corner of Davenport's. Seeing them, Mac bent over to help his wife. "Oh, did you slip and fall, my dear?"

The Marshes asked if she needed help, but she didn't. Not even with the blood running from her ear. The MacGregors lived only two blocks east on Villard, so when they left with Mac's arm around Ethelene, the Marshes weren't too concerned.

At the alley, they met Art, who told them what he had seen. The news spread pretty fast once Mrs. Marsh got to her telephone. Women called other women; wives talked to husbands; daughters to fathers; sisters to brothers.

Wednesday evenings were set aside for Prayer Meetings in the various Protestant churches. Ethelene left her house and walked alone to her church. Fifteen minutes after she left, Mac heard a knock at the back door.

When he opened it, a masked figure knocked him to the floor. Other masked men entered the house. Mac didn't have a chance.

When Ethelene came home, Mac was nursing a split lip, broken nose, blackening eye, and a cracked rib. Ethelene doctored the wounds as best she could. Mac thanked her.

He never touched her in anger again.

But Alv wasn't physically violent; his emotional abuse reduced Tina in a wholly different way. Lacking affection and even common human sympathy from her husband, her spirit just ebbed away.

Her mother and sisters saw her condition, but she wouldn't discuss it with any of them, and if they persisted, just sat still and would not say a word.

With the Eighteenth Amendment and the Volstead Act, the entire United States went "dry." What had been a local and state enforcement issue, now became federal.

Alv had always gotten along with the local enforcers and would pay his fine whenever they had to make a show for the community. At first, he worked the same arrangement with the federal man, Peter Brooks, and everything went smoothly.

Then one day when it was Alv's turn to be the semi-monthly example and pay a fine, he rebelled and socked Brooks on the jaw. Alv's blacksmith power knocked Brooks out and when he came to, he preferred charges. Alv ended up in jail for ten days.

Brooks said that if he ever caught Alv drinking again, he'd haul him in on federal charges and the same for any blind pig who served him.

It was just before Thanksgiving that Alv started his ten days. Tina was baking some traditional Norwegian cookies for the holiday, and lots of them because some would go to her family and some to the church supper. She was making pepperkaker, a gingerbread cookie; krumkaker, which would be delicious filled with whipped cream; kokosmakroner, a coconut macaroon; and sandkake, a simple, flat, baked short cake.

She hadn't been feeling very well, no energy, and the blood

spotting bothered her. Her abdomen was hurting more and more, but she thought it would pass after the stress of the holidays was over.

Just as she took some sandkake from the oven, she bent over with pain, the sandkake molds falling to the floor. She made it to bed and tried to overcome the pain by thinking of the coming good times she was going to have with her mother and sisters and their families. When the thoughts didn't work, she prayed. When the pain didn't lessen, she called her mother, who called Doc Blanchard, who lived in the Oleson House just a block away.

Doc asked her some questions and looked very serious. He was especially worried about the blood. He pressed and prodded her abdomen. Her mother arrived just as he was finishing. Doc asked to use the phone.

Soon Dr. Lee showed up. He checked Tina's abdomen, then he and Doc Blanchard conferred in the living room. Before they left, they gave Tina some medicine for the pain.

Alone, Tina drifted back to being a little girl when she dreamed of her wedding day where she would have a kransekake made from almonds, sugar, and egg whites and stacked in concentric rings with white icing holding them together and drizzled with white glaze. A little figure of a bride dressed in white was on top. It was funny, but she never saw a groom's figure there. It must have been a premonition because Alv didn't want any frills at the wedding.

In her mind, she and her new husband would lift the top ring and however many rings came with it would be the number of children they'd have. Sometimes it was three, sometimes four, but that never worked out for her, either.

The next day the two doctors and a doctor from Caseyville came to the house. The Caseyville doctor went through the same routine. When they had finished, they asked to see Tina's mother, who had stayed overnight, in the living room. They gave her the bad new—a tumor, undoubtedly malignant, too far gone, patient wouldn't withstand operation anyway, terribly sorry.

The Caseyville doctor withdrew; Dr. Lee told Tina, with Doc Blanchard holding her crying mother.

Her mother and sisters took care of her; she never complained about the pain or about the unfairness. The day Alv was released, she passed away, thinking of her white wedding cake decorated with a little white figure on top and small Norwegian flags on the sides. Slowly the wedding cake dissolved and was gone.

Alv was useless as to funeral arrangements, so Tina's family took over.

Alv was sober as he sat in the front pew with his in-laws. His head was in his hands and he kept moaning loud enough to be heard, "My Angel; My Angel." One of Tina's sisters put her arm around him, but he would not be comforted.

He spent Christmas with Tina's family, and, while he wasn't the life of the party, at least he was pleasant to everyone and thanked them as he left.

Then he got down to work.

Mrs. Flaherty, who lived across the street, kept her friends informed about the work going on in Alv's shop, not just the daily repair work, but something else behind a large piece of canvas in a corner of the building that he wouldn't let anyone see.

Alv bought a burial plot in the far northwestern corner of Eternal Rest Cemetery. There were no graves within fifty yards.

Tina's body had been kept in a vault over the winter months; no one could chop through the frozen Dakota soil to make a grave. In the spring the gravedigger got busy; several other people had passed away during the long dormant months.

Many of the ladies from town and a few of Alv's friends were at the committal services in late April. Alv was pleasant to them and thanked them for coming. They could see how he had been redeemed, even though it was too late for Tina.

Alv carved a grave marker himself; it read KRISTINA A. ANDREASSEN; below that 1895-1921; and near the bottom MY ANGEL. He set it in place himself. Upon first seeing it, several women burst into tears.

Next Alv went to the Ladies' Cemetery Auxiliary for a variance on their rules governing the size of tombstones and grave markers.

When he proposed one that would stand at least three feet higher than what was allowed, the ladies went into executive session, where they were split into two groups; the traditionalists and the sentimentalists.

The traditionalists were opposed to granting any variance; they thought uniformity made for a better look in the cemetery. The sentimentalists agreed as far as aesthetics, but they made a case for Alv, based on his change of heart: they did not wish to do anything that would discourage him from continuing to be the sort of man he had become: diligent, sober, respectful, and one who no longer used curse words.

The power of sympathy won over the edicts of reason; Alv got busy.

Over the next few days he drove out to Eternal Rest and dug a hole a couple feet deep and a yard square. He threw coarse gravel on the bottom. He pounded together a wooden form and secured it around the perimeter of the hole. The top of the form was about a foot above the surface of the soil.

He unloaded a mud box and poured in some cement and screened gravel, then he used a mortar hoe to mix it all together. He made several trips to the cemetery pump, filling buckets with water, and lining them up near his work site.

He mounded his concrete mixture, made a depression in the top, and added some water. He used the hoe to push the wet mixture to the sides of the box. He added more water and continued to mix until he was satisfied with the consistency. Then he poured and mixed, poured and mixed, until he had enough wet concrete.

He used a shovel to ladle the mixture into the hole, stopping every so often to tamp it with a broom handle.

When he was finished, he used a trowel to level it and smooth it, flicking away a couple large stones that appeared near the surface. He measured carefully and placed four heavy bolts upside down in the cement, smoothed the surface again, stood up, and smiled.

Every day a representative of the Ladies' Auxiliary was in Eternal Rest, ostensibly to care for some neglected graves, but really to keep an eye on Alv. When the rest of the ladies heard the glowing reports of how hard Alv was working to build a monument to his poor wife, the traditionalists went over to the side of the sentimentalists.

Mrs. Flaherty reported that her sources—the men who exited Alv's shop after giving him some work to do—told her Alv was not doing stone carving as he had for Tina's gravestone. He was doing some kind of metal working, using his big furnace to melt something, probably iron. He had forms in which to pour the liquid metal. Some were maybe eight feet long, but Alv kept them under a canvas, so that was a guess.

Later in the spring Alv, Ole Skogen, and Thor Wahlberg loaded his Nash two-ton with several pieces and his acetylene unit and went out to Eternal Rest. Ole and Thor held the pieces in place while Alv welded them together. Two large nuts were screwed onto each of the bolts which thrust up through the base of the new statue.

The men stood back and admired their work. Proudly standing on its concrete platform was a ten-foot iron figure with wings outspread. Near the bottom of its flowing robe appeared a metal plaque with "MY ANGEL." And that was exactly what the statue was.

When the ladies of the Auxiliary checked it out, they couldn't believe how much the face resembled Tina. Alv's sins were completely washed away.

He almost became a saint when people noticed he would go out nearly every day and kneel in front of the statue.

When he went to the Auxiliary and asked permission to erect a wind break, the vote was unanimous in favor.

Some people thought it strange when he put the wooden fence on the south and east sides of the grave because the prevailing winds were from the northwest, but the doubters wisely never told any ladies of their doubts.

Sainthood was confirmed on Alv after it was noticed several times a week he would spend an hour or two in a chair behind the wind break. He was truly showing his wife to be an angel.

Once Peter Brooks pulled Alv over as he drove to Eternal Rest, but found nothing in the vehicle. So many ladies complained to his bosses, that Brooks never dared do that again.

Although Alv continued to do some work in his shop as the years passed, it was noted that he was becoming more and more erratic. He was also aging considerably. He was in his thirties, but looked older than fifty. Liquor was suspected.

There were two major blind pigs in town and several minor ones. The two biggest were Doc Carlson, who ran a place on St. Paul, and Tillie Mortensen, who peddled booze just across the alley from the jail and would drive her 250-lb. frame home in a Packard "Twin Six" Coupe.

Peter Brooks constantly checked out the pigs, but all of them denied supplying Alv with any alcohol. They knew Brooks would come down hard on anyone who violated the Volstead Act by selling to him.

Over five years had passed after the erection of the Angel before Alv's secret was known, but the secret sharers were too afraid to say anything.

One June, Widow Potman's youngest boys, Henry George and Thomas Woodrow Potman, asked their mother if they could go on a nature hike. She thought it a good idea, but they had to promise to stay south of the Jacques River. They promised.

She packed each of them a lunch, they filled their canteens with water, and off they went two blocks to the NP tracks and then north to the railroad bridge. They climbed on the wooden supports and pilings of the bridge for awhile, sat on the edge and watched the water, and eventually got bored.

In the way of young boys, they began to dare each other to cross the bridge to the north side of the river. Henry George, being the older, was the first one to venture beyond his mother's instructions. Seeing him on the other side of the water, Thomas Woodrow scampered after.

They went down into the reeds and flushed out a pair of teal, who flew off upriver, sounding their displeasure. They looked into the culvert under the gravel road; it was half full of mud and debris. Again boredom set in.

Off to the north, they saw the trees marking Eternal Rest. Henry

George said, "Let's go visit Papa." So away they went, walking the rails that ran north straight as two dark strings. The ditches along the right-of-way had some water and rushes; the boys scared up a couple mallards, but mostly it was dry along the railroad. A jack rabbit bolted out of the ditch, went under the barbed wire fence, and headed west through a pasture, brown fur and long legs running under the black-tipped jackass ears.

Thomas Woodrow kept looking back at the shrinking town, but Henry George marched a determined pace. Whenever a vehicle appeared on the road to their right, they went down the other side of the right-of-way and remained hidden until it passed. A mile later they turned onto a gravel road and walked into Eternal Rest. The cloudless day had warmed; there was no one else around. They found their father's grave and looked down at the stone with his name, dates, and "PEACE" carved on it. They bowed their heads, clasped their hands, and said "little boy" prayers.

They were hungry and wanted a nice place to sit while they ate. They walked out to Tina's grave and sat on the cement base. They unwrapped their peanut butter and jelly sandwiches and took out apples and bananas, placing them on the waxed paper from the sandwiches. After the meal there were peanuts, unsalted in the shell, which they put in their mouths, split open with their teeth, and chewed. They made certain the shells went into the paper bags.

Thomas Woodrow wanted to go back; he was afraid that someone might see them and tell their mother. Henry George would like to have stayed and explored, but he felt a twinge of conscience about his disobedience, so he agreed they'd head back. They went into the tall grass and trees to the north and obeyed the "call of nature."

Finished, they walked toward Eternal Rest and stopped short. A large dark car was turning in. It slowly drove around the cemetery. It was the only vehicle. It stopped to the south of MY ANGEL and Tillie Mortensen got out.

The two boys got down on hands and knees and crawled as close to the edge of the trees as they dared. They parted the grass and watched. Tillie was carrying a bag. It seemed heavy. She stopped in front of MY ANGEL and gave a look around.

Henry George said, "We forgot our bags." Panic set in. They could see the two crumpled bags and their canteens on the cement.

Tillie apparently didn't see them or didn't care. She knelt on the concrete, reached for the plaque, and, to the amazement of the boys, swung it open. She took out an envelope, counted something inside, and took three empty bottles out of the statue. After she placed three full bottles in the statue, she put the empties in her bag and pushed herself up.

She looked around and, apparently satisfied, walked to the Packard "Twin Six" Coupe. After the car disappeared in the dust of the gravel road, the boys hightailed it to MY ANGEL, grabbed their stuff, and ran back into the trees.

They were so nervous they had to go find a spot to relieve themselves again. When they returned to their sacks and canteens, a Model T was stopping just where Tillie had parked. Alv got out and walked to MY ANGEL. He knelt, put his hands together, and appeared to be praying. He pulled open the plaque and brought out a bottle, looked around, sat in the chair, and began to drink.

Mesmerized, the two boys would have stayed in their hidden vantage point to see how much Alv would put away, but Thomas Woodrow noticed some dark lines wriggling toward them over the cemetery grass. When it turned into a garter snake, the boys crawled and then ran to the north side of the trees. They walked to the NP and headed south, making certain to walk in the west ditch several hundred yards, so Alv couldn't see them.

At home when Mrs. Potman asked about their hike, they told her it was the most interesting one they'd ever taken.

Alv slowly deteriorated as the years crept by. His business went downhill until even his sober periods couldn't save it. He stayed home more and more, only venturing out to Eternal Rest until his Model T broke down.

Mrs. Flaherty could hear him at night. She thought it was the D.T.'s, but just told her friends that Alv had bad dreams.

One day Alv showed up at Tillie's, looking for a drink and wearing just a bathrobe and old boots. The sheriff took him to the State Asylum in Kingston, where he died after a few weeks.

Six months later the Twenty-First Amendment repealed Prohibition.

In the summer a violent thunderstorm hit the Menninger area. A lightning bolt hit MY ANGEL, shattering it. The wooden wind break burned to the ground. The concrete pad was shattered, and workmen were hired to remove it and all the other debris.

Orange lichen began to grow on the gravestone, covering the carving.

Many years later during a Potman reunion the family members drove to Eternal Rest to visit the graves of their parents. Their children were told to show respect to Grandma and Grandpa by not being too loud.

As the others were talking and looking at various graves, Thomas Woodrow and Henry George walked over to the northwest section, now thick with graves. They found the one they were looking for. The lichen had covered everything but "TINA A. 5-1 MY ANG."

The gravestone next to it was equally lichen-covered. It read "ALV EASS."

CAPTAIN MIDNIGHT AND THE TOM MIX RALSTON STRAIGHT SHOOTER

ittle Orphan Annie was my favorite radio show. After school on nice days, I'd play with my friends or go exploring along the railroad tracks, but on rainy or wintry days, I'd get a cookie—only one—from the cookie jar and stir chocolatey Ovaltine into a glass of milk. I'd turn on the big Zenith console radio in the living room and sit right in front of the large vertical speaker. Then, at 4:45, direct from the NBC affiliate in Fargo:

> "Who's that little chatterbox?
> The one with the pretty auburn locks?
> Whom do you see?
> It's Little Orphan Annie!"
> She and Sandy make a pair;
> They never seem to have a care!
> Cute little she;
> It's Little Orphan Annie!"

For the next fifteen minutes I'd be with Annie, her dog Sandy, her friend Joe Corntassel, and sometimes her capitalist friend Oliver "Daddy" Warbucks and his servant, the giant Indian Punjab, fighting pirates, smugglers, crooks, kidnappers, and gangsters.

At the end of the program, there was an announcement of how to get the latest Annie premium—a decoder pin, a magnifying ring, a shake-up mug, a Secret Society coin, small things to get a boy's heart pumping. I even sent in ten cents and some aluminum strip seals from the Ovaltine can to get a ring, which I promptly lost along the railroad tracks.

Then one January afternoon Annie was gone. I searched the dial for a week with no luck. When spring came, I had lost interest in radio—I wandered the town and played countless hours with friends. The summer days waxed and waned.

A September rain drove me indoors. I saw the Zenith, its brown wood shining because of my mother's care. I turned it on and sat down, twisting the dial until from Station KRSW in Sacred Water:

A church bell slowly tolled midnight. An airplane dove out of the sky. Using an echo chamber, announcer Pierre Andre, a holdover from *Little Orphan Annie* so I knew his voice, opened a program I'd never heard:

> "Cappp-taaiinn Midnight!
> Brought to you every day...Monday through Friday...
> By the makers of Ovaltime!"

It was explained that Captain Midnight had been sent on a mission in France during World War I; his superiors thought it was a suicide run, but the Captain's plane came thundering back at midnight, after successfully saving France. Over the next twenty years whenever a trouble spot developed anywhere in the world, a mysterious plane would roar through a night sky, and Captain Midnight would appear to fight evil, often in the form of Ivan Shark, his daughter Fury, or the "Barracuda." The Captain would be aided by members of his Secret Squadron—Kelly, Chuck Ramsey, Joyce Ryan, and Ichabod "Ichy" Mudd, their mechanic.

I didn't spend all my time in front of the Zenith; I liked being outdoors, but then I found out that Timmy Corcoran liked radio heroes, too.

Timmy was new. Old Hans Vogler, who ran a shoe shop over on

Dunnell, was suffering more and more from rheumatism, especially in cold weather, of which we in Menninger, North Dakota, had plenty. He hired Michael Corcoran to do most of the shoe repairs and leather work, while he handled the business end. The Corcorans moved into a two-story white house a couple block east of the shoe shop after school began.

About the third week of school, we were seated in alphabetical order, except for Peter Adair, who had trouble seeing the board and was in a special desk in the front of the room. His parents had been trying to save enough money for glasses, but with seven kids they didn't have any luck.

I was in the first row against the windows: it started with Anderson and ended with Dillon. I was Coughlin so I was in the second desk to the last. Timmy was put in front of me which moved everyone back one in all the rows. Most of them liked where they had been, so they didn't like Timmy. I was ecstatic because Benny Dillon would tug on my hair or snap my ears with his finger when the teacher wasn't looking, and I knew if I turned around to get him back, the teacher would certainly see me, and I'd be the one punished.

Timmy was by far the smallest in our class; even "Little Alice" had him by an inch. He had red hair, cut short; light skin with small freckles; and blue-green eyes. His short legs made him a slow runner, so he wasn't much good at tag ("Last one down there's 'It'" and he was always the last one), and his small frame made him the last to be chosen for our recess games of touch football. If the teachers hadn't told us everyone had to be chosen, he and Peter would have been perpetual spectators.

I didn't say a word to him the first week he was in school.

I lived three blocks from the school on Oakes Avenue. In good weather I'd head for home to eat dinner, but if it rained, snowed, or they had something extra good for school lunch, I ate in the lunch room. Timmy either ate out of a paper bag packed at home or walked to Dunnell and over to his house.

The next week I found myself walking next to him south on the sidewalk paralleling Salem Street. At first nothing. Then I said, "Like it here?"

He hesitated. "It's all right."

"Where you from?"

"Milwaukee."

"Wisconsin?"

"Yeah."

And that was our first conversation, but I did say "Hi" to him on the playground that afternoon at recess. He was waiting a turn on the monkey bars. He looked at me and said, "Hi."

The next noon we were walking beside each other again. We had crossed Villard and hadn't spoken. I got nervous and blurted out, "D'ya like Captain Midnight?"

"He's O.K., but my favorite is Tom Mix."

The *Tom Mix and the Ralston Straight Shooters* program came over the NBC Blue Network at the same time *Captain Midnight* was on and was opposite *Little Orphan Annie* before that, so I hadn't listened to it much.

It began with the sounds of Tom riding his horse Tony. There would be a whinny and then "Up, Tony!...come on, boy!" and Tom would sing:

> "Shre-ea-ded Ralston for your breakfast,
> Starts the day off shining bright;
> Gives you lots of cowboy energy,
> With a flavor that's just right!
> It's delicious and nutritious,
> Bite-size and ready to eat;
> Take a tip from Tom,
> Go and tell your Mom,
> Shredded Ralston can't be beat!"

From the little I'd listened to, I didn't think it was as exciting as *Captain Midnight*, but to keep the conversation going, I said, "Maybe you'd like to come over and listen someday."

Timmy gave a little smile. "O.K."

He didn't come over right away, but we did start to talk more at school. The reason he hadn't come over was because he knew *Captain Midnight* and *Tom Mix* were on at the same time, and he didn't want me to miss my program. And he admitted he didn't want to miss his. We decided to compromise: one afternoon Captain and the next Tom.

When Timmy showed up the next day, he was wearing a black ten-gallon hat that was so big only his ears kept it from covering up his face. We listened to *Tom Mix* and his cowboy adventures, and I got increasingly jealous of Timmy's hat.

After he left, I hustled up to the attic and went through a trunk until I found an old brown leather aviator's cap that had belonged to Uncle Howard when he was much younger. It looked like one of those I had seen in a picture of "Lucky Lindy." When I put it on, it was only a little too big, and I liked the way the straps felt on my cheeks, just the way Captain Midnight must have felt in the cap I imagined him wearing.

The next afternoon both of us wore our headgear as we listened to Captain Midnight. When Mom brought us glasses of Ovaltine and milk and a peanut butter cookie each, it was a perfect afternoon.

A week or so later I found Timmy crying behind the caragana bushes that bordered the east side of the school playground. When he had come into the room that morning and sat down, I had noticed his eyes were red, but I thought he had a cold or something.

"What's wrong?"

"Tom's dead." His eyes began leaking. He wiped them with his sleeve.

"Who's dead?"

"Tom Mix. My Dad heard it on the radio."

I couldn't think of anything to say. I just put my arm around his thin shoulders while he kept his head down so none of the other kids would see him cry.

That was a bum day in school.

Sure enough when the *Fargo Forum* came up on the train there was the story. Tom Mix, 60, had been killed in a traffic accident in

Arizona when his car went off the highway while he was attempting to stop for some barricades marking a washed-out bridge.

For a couple days Timmy and I didn't speak much, then he came up to me before the morning bell and said, "He's still on."

"Who?"

"Tom Mix."

"But he's dead."

"But he's on the radio."

And he was. For the first time in a week, we listened at my house and there he was, Tom Mix, sounding just the same as he beat the bad guys again.

That was strange, Tom Mix dead, but alive, too. I knew that radio characters like the Shadow and the Green Hornet weren't real, and comic book heroes like Superman, the Human Torch, the Flash, and Sub-Mariner were too fantastic to be real, but I wasn't too sure that Batman in the comics and Captain Midnight, Jack Armstrong, and Renfrew of the Mounted on radio weren't real people. Tom Mix was dead, but he was still on the radio; it was a real puzzle.

I wouldn't say that Timmy was my best friend. There were three that I chummed around with: Andy "Pinky" Black, who lived up on Tilden; Joe Ripley, whose home was across from the court house on Villard; and Hermy Ritzke, who lived across the GN tracks on Jay Cooke Avenue.

Pinky got his nickname because his ears were always pink, even when it wasn't summer. Joe's Dad Blayne and my Dad both worked for the Melva Cunningham Contracting Company, so they went out on the road together in the spring and came back in the late fall. Hermy's Dad was dead. He had been one of the garbage men in town, but the only one who still used a horse and wagon. Working in the cold was not good for his lungs. Sometimes I'd see him loading ashes and refuse from our pile by the garage and then head out to the garbage dump east of town, puffing on a cigarette and coughing. He'd been dead five years, but his horse was still alive. Sometimes Pinky, Joe, and I would go down to Hermy's place set back in some box elders so it was hard to see from the street. We'd ride his horse around the barnyard, scattering the chickens, a couple cows, and pigs out of the way. We liked Hermy even if he didn't have a Dad.

For the past several years the four of us would go out trick-or-treating together. That year I talked the others into letting Timmy come along. We didn't dress up much: Pinky, Joe, and I had cheap dime store masks, and Hermy put on one of his Dad's old work shirts and caps, rubbed dirt on his face, and came as a tramp. When Timmy showed up, he had on his black cowboy hat, a bandana around his neck, and a black mask over his eyes like the Lone Ranger wore in the comic strips. From their comments I could tell the others approved and I was glad.

We walked over to Villard and began knocking on doors. Our bags were pretty full by the time we got too cold to keep going. The richer people in Menninger showed off their generosity and maintained their status in our eyes with their candy bars, instead of the penny candy you'd get in other neighborhoods.

We filled our bags with O'Henrys, Charleston Chews, Baby Ruths, Milky Ways, Mr. Goodbars, Squirrel Nut Zippers, Snickers, Valomilks, and Sky Bars, as well as Necco Wafers and Dum Dums. If we got a Mounds, it went into the nearest bushes since none of us liked coconut. Timmy hadn't gone trick or treating in Milwaukee, so he couldn't get over how easy it was. His enthusiasm spilled over onto us and it became the best Halloween ever.

After we got to be better friends and before the snow blanketed everything, a typical Saturday for us would be to walk down Dunnell to Vogler's Shoe Shop, where Timmy's Dad would be working. I liked the leather-smell of the place, not just the shoes and boots, but the tack hanging down and the saddles placed on supports like saw-horses.

Sometimes Mr. Corcoran would swing Timmy into one saddle and me into another and laugh when we pretended to be Tom Mix and my favorite cowboy, the Cisco Kid, that I'd seen in movies at the Blackstone Theatre on Chicago.

The saddles would make little creaking leathery sounds as we stood in the stirrups and pretended to be riding. Sometimes Mr. Vogler would come out from the back and smile.

The big white and green Melva Cunningham Contracting Company garage and repair shop was right across the street. We'd walk over and get my Dad's attention. Just because there was no road work didn't mean the employees were idle. The graders, trucks, and all the earth moving and road construction equipment had to be repaired and fixed up for the coming spring. The sounds of welding, pounding, and metal falling on the concrete floor echoed off the ceiling.

Dad wouldn't have much time to talk, but it was enough for me to see him and say hello because he was gone so much.

We'd cross St. Paul and wave at Floyd Freye, the big sandy-haired manager of the elevator that stood on a spur line of the NP. He lived across the alley from the Corcorans. He'd give us a huge smile and a wave; everyone liked Floyd.

Sometimes we'd stop at the Amalgamated Farmers' Station on the corner of Chicago and Dunnell, especially if Dad had given us money for a pop. Other times we'd just go in and listen to the men talk about farm prices, the weather, and the latest policy of the federal government.

Then it was down Dunnell again. Off to our left was the long, low, gray Gustavus Turkey Processing Plant and on our right stood the Plymouth-Dodge Garage.

Crossing Dakota Street, we kept our eyes peeled for any trains on the GN and birds or muskrats on the marsh to our south, or for Hedy Vogler in the house near the corner. We'd make sure to walk slow because if she saw us, she'd come out with two of the biggest chocolate chip cookies, hold them out, and smile. We liked Hedy.

She was no relation to Hans Vogler. I thought for a long time she was a widow, but my mother told me she had a husband some place and wouldn't go into any detail. Her daughter Maggie Chambers lived up on the corner of Dakota and Stimson. Her husband Dick worked for Melva Cunningham. They had two kids, a boy and a little baby girl. All the Cunningham wives got together and gave them a shower when the baby was born. Mom went.

We'd walk by the marsh and dare each other to cross the foot bridge that led to the rail yards, but we were too chicken or just too young.

One winter evening I was thinking about Mrs. Vogler and then it dawned on me that maybe Timmy's mother was dead or gone away because I had never seen her.

I said, "Mom, is Timmy's mother dead?"

My Dad was on the couch, with the *Reader's Digest*. He said, "Well, if she keeps going uptown at night, she'll find it in a bottle."

"James, don't! Little pitchers have big ears!...Junior, don't listen to your father. Yes, Timmy has a mother. She just doesn't get out much; she's been ill."

Dad cleared his throat in a faked-up kind of way. Mom glared at him over the ironing she was doing.

My Dad was James Coughlin, Sr. I was James, Jr., so everyone called me "Junior." I liked that because I wanted to be just like my Dad.

"Is she gonna die?"

"No. No, of course not."

There was a long silence, then I told them about a big squirrel I had seen in the Bakers' yard.

Winter weather kept us closer to home and closer to the radio, but the next spring Timmy and I were out exploring again, getting farther and farther away. As long as we stayed on the south side of Lamborn, I knew I was O.K., but three blocks north of Lamborn was the Jacques River, and Mom would skin me alive if she found out that I had gone anywhere near the water. Timmy didn't seem to have any limits, so mine became his.

We decided that we should have adventures just like Captain Midnight and Tom Mix, and the best places were the marshes along the two railroads and the railroads themselves. We'd walk along the marshes, looking for signs of a struggle, the tracks of a bear or other dangerous beasts, maybe the body of a tramp who had been thrown off a freight.

The only things we found that summer were some rusty railroad spikes and my old Orphan Annie magnifying ring.

We had been walking down Salem past our neighbors to the south, the Bakers, kicking stones sticking out of the gravel into the ditch. We'd reached the tracks. Suddenly, Timmy yelled and reached into the ballast. He came up with my Orphan Annie magnifying ring, which I had lost walking to Hermy's house.

What could I say? "Hey, that's my ring!" He wouldn't believe that, and there'd be an argument and hurt feelings whoever won, so I let it go.

The only thing was he started wearing the ring all the time and seeing what was actually mine rubbed me the wrong way.

That didn't stop our friendship. Our searches for summer adventures continued, fruitless though they were.

In the fall our radio afternoons resumed, as did school, football, and cooler weather. Then on Sunday, December 7, 1941, Pearl Harbor. Then President Roosevelt asked for a declaration of war against Japan. Hitler declared war on us; everything changed.

Radio changed. War bulletins broke in. War news dominated. President Roosevelt reassured. Some of my parents' favorite shows, such as *Fibber McGee and Molly* and *The Bob Hope Show*, carried patriotic themes. Suddenly, spies were everywhere. *Counterspy* joined the Blue Network; its star David Harding took on the German Gestapo and the Japanese Black Dragon. (Mom didn't like me to listen because the sponsor was Mail Pouch Tobacco.)

One Saturday night a year before the Corcorans moved to town, my parents and I were walking by the Blackstone Theatre when I saw a poster with an actor named Edward G. Robinson with his arm around a man in a brown suit and pointing a finger toward the man's face. The movie was *Confessions of a Nazi Spy*. If Hollywood knew there were spies, who was I not to believe in them.

The Nakamura family owned the Menninger Café. A few weeks after Pearl Harbor, Timmy came up to me in school and said he'd seen a Japanese man at the post office, picking up a package. He was sure he was a spy.

After talking with Timmy, I knew the "spy" was Yoshiro Nakamura. I tried to convince him all the Nakamuras were loyal Americans, but he wouldn't be persuaded.

I talked with Mom and Dad, and we decided to take Timmy out for Sunday dinner at the Menninger Café. Yoshiro and his wife Sumiko were in the kitchen, but would occasionally come out and greet a diner or stop by a booth to see how the food was. Their two children, Taro and Katsumi, waited tables. After Timmy saw the Nakamuras working, being friendly, and speaking English with just a bare hint of an accent, he believed like the rest of us that they were good people. After Yashiro was arrested and taken to the Ft. Lincoln internment camp south of Bismarck, Timmy helped circulate petitions for his release, which was granted a couple months later.

After the release the Nakamuras, Japanese-Americans, and Hans Vogler, German-American, became very active in the various drives to save grease, rubber, scrap metal, and other things useful to the war effort.

With the Nakamuras safely identified as good Americans, there were no more spies in Menninger. Timmy and I listened to the radio, but after March, Tom Mix disappeared, so Timmy had to listen to Captain Midnight.

We thought of going out to track down spies, but what self-respecting spy would walk around Menninger in the snow. He would leave tracks and the authorities would nab him. Besides, most of the time it was too cold for us to go spy-chasing.

After the snow melted and the sun was on its return north, it was a different story. We decided to trail spies, report them, and become heroes.

At first, we'd go out on Saturdays and Sundays, walking the tracks and looking for places where spies had loosened a rail so the train would crash. We went out more often after school got out.

Sometimes we'd be walking the NP rails on the lookout for loose rails, broken ties, maybe even dynamite, anything spies might do, and we'd see Tommy Cockburn and Bobby Swain collecting old tires and other rubber products, scrap metal, cans, and other things that could be turned into war materiel they found in the ditches along the tracks.

They'd call for us to help, but we waved and kept going—we were doing important war work ourselves.

Eventually after not finding any sabotage in the area, we decided that any real spy would operate at night, so we began sneaking out after dark. Timmy's bedroom window opened right onto their front porch. He just opened it and stepped out. His parents slept in the back of the house, so they never heard him.

I had to open my window which was above the back entry. Then I'd climb down the trellis nailed to the wall. Mom was a heavy sleeper and never missed me.

For a couple weeks we were out 'til after midnight, walking the alleys, searching the dark areas near the two railroad depots and along the tracks. We never found anything suspicious and were ready to give up, but I said we should give it one more try. Timmy agreed and we met by the Standard Station. We checked all around the gas stations in town—Standard, Cities Service, Purol, Mobil, Amalgamated Farmers—because maybe a spy was trying to blow one up.

We didn't find a blamed thing and headed for home.

We were in Timmy's alley when I saw two figures walk into the shadows ahead. Right across from Timmy's yard was a big wooden arbor. The two people were standing in the vine-covered arbor so we couldn't see them, but we could hear their voices—one was a woman and one was a man.

I knew that women could be spies, so I whispered, "I think they might be spies."

"Yeah, maybe they are. Ain't we lucky. We might catch 'em."

"Shhhh. Sneak along this fence. Quiet, now."

We stayed in the shadows, going slowly so we didn't step on anything that would make noise. Soon the voices became more distinct.

The woman said, "I'll try again, but it's so hard to talk to him, especially about this."

"Well, I'll do it."

"No."

"I can't stand it anymore. We have to be together. I love you. You don't love him."

It sounded like they were kissing. Timmy had been a little behind me. He came up and listened.

"Do you love him?"

"Not anymore. I love you." They kissed again.

Just listening to them kiss was exciting. I whispered to Timmy, "This is better than spies."

He wasn't there. I saw him at the end of the alley. As quickly as I could, I caught up to him. He was crying. "Are you scared?"

He kept crying.

"What's wrong?"

"Nothin'. I want to go in." He turned toward Dunnell without a word. I couldn't figure it out all the way home.

I didn't see him for a couple days. Then Hermy came over; I met him in our back yard.

"D'ja hear about Mr. Corcoran and Floyd?"

"What about 'em?"

"Well, somethin' happened that touched off Floyd. Ya know that temper o' his. He came bustin' into Old Man Vogler's shop and knocked Corcoran to the floor with a punch that broke his jaw. Corcoran had been putting on a heel, so he had his hammer. When he got up, he clobbered Floyd across the skull and knocked him out. Vogler called the cops and they both went to the hospital and then to jail."

"Are they all right?"

"If ya call a busted jaw 'all right', then Corcoran is. Floyd's in the hospital with a fractured skull."

"Is he gonna die?"

"Naw. He's got a thick head. Guess who went up right away to visit him?"

"I don't know."

"Mrs. Corcoran."

"Naw, she never goes out."

"Well, she did and Corcoran wasn't too happy. Despite his jaw, they had a terrible fight, the neighbors said."

Hermy asked me if I wanted to go catch frogs in the railroad ditch, but I didn't feel like it.

The next day Mom and I walked uptown to the IGA store. I liked walking with her in the sunshine, carrying the cloth grocery bags we would fill. We'd talk about people in town, favorite songs, what was going to happen next on *I Love a Mystery*, all kinds of good things.

As we were checking out, Mrs. Brennan got very confidential. She made certain I couldn't hear her whisper, but my hearing must have been sharper than she realized, or her voice louder. She said that Mr. Corcoran had found out something about his wife and blackened her eyes and bloodied her nose. The only reason he wasn't up on charges was that the Corcorans were leaving town.

Walking home wasn't as much fun. I didn't have much to say.

After we put away the groceries, I asked Mom if I could say goodbye to Timmy. She hesitated, but when she saw how much I wanted to, she let me go.

I knocked on the back door a couple times before a woman answered. She was thin, had dishwater blonde hair, and sported two dark eyes.

"Hello."

"Hello, yourself. Whaddaya want?"

"I heard you were leaving town, so I wanted to say goodbye to Timmy. He's my friend."

"What's your name?"

"Junior…I mean Jimmy Coughlin."

"Junior, huh. So you're the brat that got me in Dutch with my husband and ruined it for me and Floyd by dragging Timmy through the alleys where he had no right to be. Get the hell off my property. Timmy ain't home." The door slammed.

It bothered me that she cursed. I'd never heard a woman curse before.

I walked to the alley, saw the arbor, and remembered the woman's

UNDER THE SIGN OF AQUARIUS

A minor occurrence in the French Wars of Religion was the killing of Jean-Auguste Bouvette, the grand patriarch of the Bouvette families. A widower three times over, he was on his way to the village to celebrate his 70th birthday, quite an accomplishment in an era noted for violent death and rampant disease.

Three soldiers, unpaid and desperate, cut the leather purse from his belt and slashed him across the abdomen. Being a Christian, he did not curse God for his fate; rather he shook his fist at the stars and sent his curse skyward. As he died amidst his dusty guts, steaming in the cold October night, light from the constellation Aquarius rained down at him.

The constellation Aquarius was known to the ancient Babylonians as representing the god Ea holding a vase overflowing with water which was associated with the devastating floods of the Tigris and Euphrates Rivers. In ancient Egypt when Aquarius placed his jar into the Nile, the annual spring flood began. Aquarius was also associated with water by the ancient Greeks, Hindus, and Chinese, often in its destructive aspects. Some families born under the water sign seemed destined to die under it. Woe to those cursed under its sign.

Antoine Etiénne Bouvette hated kids. He fenced off his property, so they couldn't trespass, and he chained ferocious dogs by his house that would chase off any kid unwary enough to pass by on a bicycle, the animals barking maniacally until jerked up short as they ran out of chain.

Through his father Pierre Baptiste, Antoine could trace his ancestry back to the sixteenth century. Pierre Baptiste could neither read nor write, but he listened to his mére, pére, grand-mére, and grand-pére tell family stories, and he remembered. On winter nights in the shack on the lower bank of the Jacques River, he repeated the stories told to him. His children listened and remembered.

France had been a mayhem of religious wars: Catholic against Huguenot; cities under siege; civilians slaughtered; priests killed; Huguenot leaders killed; in 1562 Francis, the Duc de Guise and a Catholic, was assassinated by a Huguenot. Foreign mercenaries invaded France in support of the Protestants; pro-Catholic rulers sent in their own troops. The Huguenots attempted to kidnap King Charles IX.

The royal family split into factions: some supported the Protestants and some remained loyal to the Catholic cause. In 1573 Henri, the new Duc de Guise, and his followers assassinated Admiral Gaspard de Coligny, the Huguenot leader, whose body was mutilated, hung on a gallows, and burned.

Attacks against Huguenots spread throughout the kingdom; as many as 10,000 Protestants were killed. Beginning on the eve of the Feast of Bartholomew the Apostle, the five-day killing spree became known as the St. Bartholomew's Day Massacre. It crippled Huguenot power.

In 1574 King Charles IX died; his brother was crowned King Henri III, a man with no sons. When his younger brother died, Henri de Navarre was the next in line of succession. However, as a Huguenot, he was unacceptable to the Catholic majority; conflict was inevitable, fueled by the Duc de Guise.

Fearing the rising power of the Guise family, Henri fomented a plot to assassinate the leading Catholics: Henri I, the Duc de Guise, and Charles, Cardinal de Bourbon, and the imprisonment of the Duc's son.

The Catholic League seethed with hatred for Henri and he became a marked man. In January 1589 Jacques Clément, a Dominican monk, was granted an audience with the king and then stabbed him in the spleen. Dying, King Henri begged Henri de Navarre to become a Catholic and take the reins of government to avoid a bloody civil war. However, more death and destruction followed.

Henri, realizing the hopelessness of a Protestant ever becoming the King of France, converted ("Paris is well worth a Mass."), was received into the Church in 1593, and crowned King of France in 1594. King Henri and his advisors saw the necessity of bringing peace to France and in improving the economy, decimated by war. In order to promote French unity, the Edict of Nantes was signed by Henri in April 1598. The law granted the Huguenots certain civil and religious rights, but kept the Catholic Church in control of the French government. Viewed as a victory for neither side, it still marked the end of the French Wars of Religion.

Even with France convulsed by religious hatred, the government encouraged fishermen in their quest for cod off the coast of Newfoundland.

Many of the Bouvette men would leave their small farms and villages on the Brittany Peninsula in northwestern France and gear-up on the fishing boats that sailed the gray Atlantic to the fishing grounds off Newfoundland. They found a huge demand for their catch as Roman Catholics were admonished to abstain from meat on Fridays and during Lent, but the consumption of fish was also sanctioned on the 165 meatless days of the liturgical calendar.

The Bouvette men and many other male inhabitants of Brittany were only too glad to take their chances against the ocean in search of the sometimes-elusive cod, if only to avoid service in the religious wars that had wracked France.

The French were not the first to fish the Grand Banks; the Portuguese had been there already, netting, drying their catch on the shore, doing a little mixing with the natives. The French fishermen generally dried their fish on board, so had less contact with the Indians.

Spanish and English ships also became frequent visitors to the fishing grounds.

When the French rulers finally made up their minds to pursue the course of empire as the Spanish and the Portuguese had for decades, they turned to the interior of the North American continent with the St. Lawrence as the artery of their advance.

Nor'easters, the tailing of a hurricane, leaky ships, and a ghostly ice burg emerging from a fog on a calm night led to enough briny deaths for the Bouvettes that they made for the shores of North America. Only one man drowned in the St. Lawrence. They settled in Three Rivers, Quebec.

Pushing west, the French eyed the furs of the interior. The Bouvettes eyed the money the furs represented. There were wives, intended wives, and hoped-for wives waiting in France. The men went west where the money was.

Some Bouvette men returned to France and made arrangements for their women to come to America. One of the ships foundered on the return and was never seen again.

The Sieur des Groseilliers and his brother-in-law Pierre Esprit Radisson explored the north shore of Lake Superior. Jacques de Noyon left the Superior waters, paddled and portaged up to Rainy Lake and Rainy River, completing what became known as the Grand Portage, bypassing rapids and waterfalls on the lower Pigeon River. Other voyageurs pushed up Rainy River to the Lake of the Woods and beyond, even to the Lake of the Assiniboin, later called Lake Winnipeg.

The great French colony of Canada was seized by the British during the French and Indian War, called the Seven Years' War in England. The country between Superior and Lake of the Woods became a source of conflict between the powerful Hudson's Bay Company, the North West Company, John Jacob Astor's American Fur Company, and the small XY Company.

The Bouvettes sided with the North West and traversed the border lakes country with other voyageurs, making the trees and rocks resound to their singing of the old songs from the Loire Valley.

Glinting red paddles propelled the light birchbark canoes over lakes and ponds and rivers. Strong legs and backs made the portages.

John Askin's post at the Superior end of the Grand Portage became the hub for the North West Company's supply route. Other companies also utilized it. Each July saw a gathering of traders, voyageurs, and trappers, some of whom had taken pelts from the mighty Oregon, later called the Columbia, or skinned the Arctic fox.

The Bouvette men powered and portaged supplies up the Grand Portage and brought furs back down. A post was established at Rainy Lake, and some of the Bouvettes became a specialized group that serviced the Athabaska trappers and traders who came there from lands hundreds of miles to the northwest.

In the summer some of the Bouvettes would head out onto the big lake and paddle all the way to the St. Lawrence Valley and their families. There they would remain, one year, two years, repairing things, learning to live again with wives and children, and, hopefully, planting the seed of new generations of Bouvettes. Superior storms clawed several canoes to the bottom. A group of Bouvettes moved further west, joining with the metis buffalo hunters around Pembina. They proved their worth, not so much with the gun, but with the knife as skinners.

During the winters they lived on the edges of the Red River Settlement and returned to the rambling life of the hunters in the summer, although the herds had been thinned and were much further south.

A dry period, including a drought in 1822 and 1823, ended and a wet period began. Heavy rains in 1824 produced minor river flooding. In 1825 there were spring and summer floods. Late storms filled every low place. The rivers froze in late October. A huge December blizzard blanketed the land. Deep snow and bitter cold drove the buffalo away and people in Pembina were starving. In 1826 spring snows, some heavy, some light, continued. The Red River did not start to break up until May 5. Tributaries poured in water. Jammed with ice dams downstream, the Red expanded upward and outward rapidly. Too rapidly for some. One Bouvette family was trapped, drowned.

After the flood subsided, the Red River Settlement moved further downstream. The Bouvettes moved, too. Winnipeg began to grow. Some Bouvettes adapted to city life. Others moved to the west. Some to the south. Some became farmers. Or worked on the railroads.

A few couldn't adapt. Antoine's father, Pierre Baptiste, could not. He and his family "crossed the line" into the United States, where he began eking out a living by trapping the scattered tributaries of the Red, and then moving further west and doing the same in the Divide and the Jacques valleys.

His family lived in a ramshackle cabin of burr oak with a sod roof on a shelf overlooking the Jacques. They lived on perch, pike, bull heads, carp, frog legs, turtle, an occasional duck or goose, rabbit, muskrat (which tasted like livery rabbit), a beaver tail once, deer if Pierre Baptiste got lucky, buffalo berries after the frost had sweetened them a bit, chokecherries, Juneberries, wild plums, and prairie roots.

After Pierre Baptiste sold some furs and pelts in the new town of Caseyville, his wife had flour to make bread.

After two of the children died, their graves were dug in the prairie. A week later Antoine and his mother went out to see them and to pray. Coyotes had torn open the graves and ravished their contents. Cloth and bones were scattered over a wide area.

Antoine and his mother gathered the remnants and buried them close to the cabin.

One autumn day when Antoine was twelve, his mother and sisters walked over to a neighbor's place to visit with the farm wife, Sarah Cotton. The two quarters the farmer and his wife had homesteaded included the piece where the Bouvette family lived, but the farmer's wife insisted they not be kicked off.

Pierre Baptiste was off hunting coyotes and figuring out where he would put his traps after winter set in. Antoine was supposed to watch his three-year old brother. The Jacques had fallen during the summer and fall, so they walked out on some mud, and Antoine filled a bucket with water. Back on the bank he told little Jean-Pierre to stay put while he went to water the flowers on the two graves.

Jean-Pierre followed a frog hopping on the mud, got to the water's

34

edge, and fell in. When Antoine came around the corner of the cabin, he saw his brother's body floating face down around a bend. He raced ahead of the body and ran onto the mud, which was strong enough to support him until he stepped into the water, where it got spongy and gummy. He went in up to his knees and could only work himself loose after ten minutes of struggling.

By the time he reached his brother, caught up in some reeds, it was too late, although Antoine tried to get him to breathe.

When his mother and sisters returned, Antoine and his brother were gone. Frantic, his mother ran back to the neighbor's farm, where Mr. Cotton organized a search. Horse-drawn wagons and buggies and men on horseback searched the area in vain.

Sixteen miles away, Antoine showed up on Main Street in Caseyville. He had something in a flour sack he carried on his back. The chief of police was called to check on the wild boy, dressed in skins and rags, walking on scratched and bloody bare feet.

Pierre Baptiste spoke no English although his wife and daughters were picking it up fairly well from their visits; Antoine knew a few words.

When the police chief attempted to take the sack, Antoine whipped out a hunting knife and threatened him. The chief easily disarmed him, but the sack fell onto the wooden sidewalk. Antoine sat down and hugged it to his body; his tears couldn't be stopped.

The chief chose some ladies from the crowd that had gathered and through soft words and sympathy, they were able to take the sack. When the sheriff's wife opened the sack, she clutched her breast and drew back with a gasp. The chief took the sack and peered inside. He hefted the sack onto his shoulder and guided the boy to the jail.

Inside the jail, the boy kept saying, "Enterrez mon frère dans une vraie tombe, s'il vous plaît." Someone recognized it as French, and the young school teacher Miss Dixon was sent for. She was the English teacher and taught German classes, but she also knew French. She told the chief the boy wanted his brother buried in a "true" grave.

People were discussing what to do when Samuel Cotton drove down Main Street to ask for help in the search. Taken to the jail, he identified Antoine and Jean-Pierre. A small casket had been brought to the jail, and Antoine told Mr. Cotton what had happened through Miss Dixon. Mr. Cotton went back to his farm, and the next morning returned with his wife; Genevieve Bouvette; and her daughters Gabrielle, Adele, and Suzette.

They had left a note for Pierre Baptiste, hoping he would recognize its one word, "Caseyville."

After listening to the Cottons relate how the Bouvette family lived, the authorities deemed it necessary for them to live in town and for the children to attend school. Genevieve started work as a hotel chambermaid; the girls took to school immediately, even though each was the oldest student in her class; only Antoine didn't seem to fit in. After a year or so of failure, he quit school and went to work for a farmer.

Pierre Baptiste never appeared in Caseyville. The Cottons checked the shack periodically before having it torn down. Several years later and dozens of miles to the south, the remnants of a man's body was found lodged in a pile of driftwood. Never officially identified, the bones were buried in the graveyard of a country church, overlooking the Jacques. Not wishing to upset them, the authorities never informed the Bouvettes. What good would that do?

Antoine eventually got a job on the farm of Pierre Babineaux, whose land lay a few miles northwest of Menninger. Pierre liked the young man and spent time helping him with his English.

Antoine's sisters all grew up and left Caseyville: Gabrielle became a nurse, Adele a teacher, and Suzette a stenographer. Genevieve moved to Minneapolis, where she lived with Gabrielle and her family until she passed away. Antoine never saw any of them after he left Caseyville.

Pierre Babineaux was a rarity: the only Frenchman in a land settled by British Islanders, Germans, and Scandinavians. Just to the south, the Murphy farm adjoined his. Blue-eyed, freckle-faced Mary Murphy was the youngest of eight children. She developed an eye for the rather taciturn young hired man, and eventually their meetings "across the fence," at barn dances, social gatherings, and even at church (Pierre made Antoine attend) developed into a relationship, and they were married.

Pierre purchased a strip of land along the Jacques in the north part of Menninger, paid for a house, and the couple moved in. Antoine kept working for Pierre, and Mary began putting in large gardens in their backyard and west along the river, all the way to Glen Haven Street. She sold much of the garden truck to supplement their income and to help pay for a small barn Antoine wanted.

When Pierre sold out and moved to California, a stipulation was that Antoine be retained as a hired man. Knowing his reputation for hard work, the new owner readily agreed.

It took awhile, but Mary eventually became pregnant. When Bridget was born, elation thrilled through each parent, and they quickly decided they wanted a large family. Pierre, Henri, Colleen, and Yvonne followed, spaced out about every other year.

Antoine put up a high woven wire fence cutting his property off from the river and forbade his children from ever going anywhere near the water. The river garden was done away with, and the backyard garden was reduced in size. Antoine bought some Shetland ponies, goats, puppies, kittens, and chickens to keep his children occupied and cows for milk. Many of the children of Menninger also played with the animals, and Mary and Antoine would look out their windows at them and smile.

Antoine became so well-liked, people started to call him "Tony," and he was elected to the Park Board. He only served one term, however, because he tried to fence off the river from the rest of the park, and when the police chief told him to stop and he resisted, he spent a night in jail.

During an unusually cold winter, Mary developed a racking cough, and her health deteriorated slowly until she became bedridden. The doctors thought it was her heart and maybe her lungs, but didn't really know what to do for her.

When the spring came, Mary had their bed moved so she could watch all the children and the animals in the backyard. Ten-year old Bridget became a good helper.

Upriver, one of Bridget's classmates, Monte Nolan, was doing some spring exploring. It was the first nice Saturday of the season, there was over a month left of school, and the river gave him a sense of the freedom he'd feel when the term ended.

He found an old rowboat hung up on the rocks that separated the ice house pond from the rest of the river. He tugged and pushed the boat, banging the timeworn wood over the stones and into the main channel. When he climbed aboard, he saw there was a small leak, so he used the one paddle to propel the boat to the north bank, tied it up, and ran to his house for an empty coffee can. He wasn't much of a swimmer, but the boat seemed safe enough.

Using just one paddle was awkward, but the slight current helped him head down the river. He banged into the pilings of the railroad bridge, but eventually passed under. He navigated the curve to the south and then to the east and went under the Steel Bridge, bottoming out on a few rocks. The leak was a little worse.

The channel narrowed, the reeds grew thicker, and just behind the reeds stood the fence that Tony Bouvette had put up. Monte smiled as he thought of his classmate Bridget, her brothers and sisters, fenced off just like little animals.

The river widened and there were the Bouvettes, hanging onto the fence and staring at him.

"Hey, Bridget, good morning; how are ya?"

"Fine. Beautiful morning." She liked Monte; he was a "river rat" just like she was.

Pierre and Henri yelled greetings and he yelled back. The other two girls just stared, especially little Yvonne.

Monte guided the boat up to the south bank. "Why don't you come exploring with me? You can help bail."

"No, we can't leave the yard."

"Chicken." Monte flapped his arms and made chicken sounds.

"No, we just can't."

"And we ain't chickens, either," Pierre said.

"C'mon. We'll just go over to the wagon wheels on the other side and then turn around and come back. It'll be ten minutes, fifteen at the most. I need someone to bail."

Pierre said, "C'mon, Bridget, just ten minutes."

Bridget hesitated, then said, "Wait," and ran into the house. When she came back, she said her father had gone uptown and her mother was asleep, so she thought a quick boat ride would be all right. The boys climbed over the fence, Bridget handed Colleen and Yvonne to Monte, and then followed. All six of them squeezed into the boat. Being barred from the river, none of the Bouvettes could swim.

"I get to bail," Pierre said.

"Me, too." Henri didn't want to be left out.

Bridget said, "You can take turns."

Monte pushed off with the paddle and everyone settled in, talking and pointing to things on the shore. All, except Yvonne, who stared at everything, but said nothing. The boat rode very low in the water, but there were no waves.

They saw the two ancient wooden wheels sticking out of the water just off a narrow point, and Monte aimed for them. Bridget and Monte had talked almost all the way about school, their friends, the coming summer, just small talk, but still very important to both of them.

Henri wanted to touch the wheels, then so did Pierre; Monte steered closer. The boat rammed the southern wheel, the children touched it, and Monte turned to head back.

"The water's comin' in faster; I can't keep up." Henri was scared.

"Gimme that." Pierre reached for the can, but it slipped free and sank into the river.

Suddenly, a bottom board gave way, a small geyser erupted in the floor, water poured over the gunwale, and the overloaded boat sank quickly and irredeemably.

When Tony walked into the house, he thought his kids would be there; they hadn't been outside. Mary was still asleep so he went looking. They weren't anywhere in the yard; the only activity he saw was downriver where a crowd of people had gathered on a makeshift beach. As he watched, a boat pulled in and two men waded out. They picked up what appeared to be a small child and put it on the sand. He saw other things already there, but they had been covered by blankets or coats.

He climbed over the woven wire fence and loped off to the east. When people saw him coming, they became silent. The priest rushed toward him, the blackness of his clothing matched by his anguished face. "Tony, you don't...." Tony pushed past him and people gave way.

Another boat came in; another body laid out. He uncovered each face. There were five. A boy from upriver. His children. All except Yvonne. Where was she?

He fell on the sand and howled his anguish as a tortured man might.

It took two days before Yvonne's little body was found at the head of an island a half mile to the east of the drowning place.

The Catholic Church was packed and people overflowed into the churchyard. The solemn Requiem Mass began. "Requiem aeternam dona eis, Domine." The priest spoke over the grief of the parents which periodically burst forth, fracturing the ritual and forcing tears from even the most-hardened of men.

A long line of vehicles, some horse-drawn, made its way north to St. Andrew's Cemetery, where five holes had been prepared. Five caskets were lowered, one smaller than the rest. Five grave markers had been ordered, one with a little lamb on the stone. The hearses, one borrowed from Caseyville, pulled away. The spectators, some of them Protestants who had never been in a Catholic cemetery before, made a path as the black-clad parents walked to the undertaker's car. No one spoke; no one reached out to touch a shoulder or an arm. Words and gestures could never alleviate the pain of loss.

Two weeks later a smaller line accompanied a hearse north: Mary Bouvette was laid to rest. She didn't mind dying: she was going to see her children.

Tony kept working on various farms, but rarely spoke to anyone. He let the backyard grow into weeds and climate-hardened shrubs.

He got rid of the ponies, goats, puppies, kittens, and chickens, so no children would ever be tempted to get near the river from his property, but he did keep two cows for milk.

He bought a great white and black dog, a ferocious beast named Styke. It lived between the long fences that marked Tony's property between Mill Avenue and the Jacques, as did its replacements, all black and white and all named Styke. Despite the wire fence most kids were afraid to go on Mill; rumor had it Styke was a man-eater.

After his retirement, Tony lost most of his land for non-payment of taxes, so he would chain Styke next to his house. The chain allowed Styke to run partially onto both Mill and Salem and kids knew it.

Decades flowed by; Tony became old. He never lost his desire to save kids from the river until one early October night. The constellation Aquarius was visible in the southern sky. The room was dark, except for the starlight. Tony was waiting for the 10 o'clock news on his small TV set.

Then he wasn't waiting anymore.

Some families born under the water sign seemed destined to die under it. Woe to those cursed under its sign.

MAGGIE: A FINAL CHAPTER

"More coffee, Mom?"

"Yes, please."

The coffee was black and strong. Both women thought that coffee made any situation or problem better. At least they felt better after a cup or two.

"He's dying, Maggie."

"I know."

"He wants us to be there."

"I can't."

"Do you hate him that much?"

"I don't hate him anymore."

"What is it then?"

"I've forgiven him. I just can't forget."

Her mother lowered her head. A strand of gray hair fell forward; her hand pushed it back behind her ear. "I know."

"What about Johnny and Alys? He's their father, too."

"Alys doesn't remember a thing about him. What Johnny remembers is being afraid of him, of his temper. Besides they have families, youngsters, they can't afford the trip from California."

"I have a family, too."

"But it's only to Minot, a hundred miles or so. I'll buy your ticket."

"I'm not going to leave Alex and Sandra with their grandmother. Richard is still working on the road. I want to be here when they come home from school."

"It'll only be a couple days."

"Maybe. Maybe not. He's mean enough to make it last a week."

"Maggie! Such a thing to say."

"I'm sorry. That's how I get, thinking about M.F."

Hedy finished her coffee and stood up. "Well, I have to pack. Thanks for the coffee, good as always."

They walked to the door. The autumn sun was warm, but the shadows of the trees were lengthening with the season.

"Are you sure?"

"Yes. Yes, I'm sure."

Hedy moved off the low porch onto the sidewalk.

Maggie watched her mother cross Stimson Avenue and walk south on Dakota. She turned back and went to the table. She had a third cup of coffee.

After school Alex would go to football practice, and Sandra told her she'd be at marching band practice if the weather was good.

Maggie made a short grocery list and headed the two blocks to downtown Menninger. She had promised herself she would always be there when her children returned from school. Today she'd still have time to bake a batch of Toll House cookies, and they'd all have cookies and milk while they told her about their day.

Walking back from the store, carrying a small paper grocery bag with just the items she needed, she thought about Richard. He was working on a highway project for the Melva Cunningham Contracting Company in the western part of the state near Banks.

After they were first married, she had gone on the road with him. They stayed in the little trailer at the camp. She'd talk with the other wives, all older than she, all used to the dust, heat, sometimes mud, and prairie wind that made her want to scream, they were so unending.

She kept her sanity by waiting for rainy days when she and Richard would lie in the little bed and listen to the lingering rain ripple on the roof. She loved the feel of his strong arms and the strength in the muscles of his back and legs. For all that, he was a gentle man. That's what she loved the most—his gentleness. With her. With the kids.

She also loved the laughter he always brought with him.

After she got pregnant, she never went on the road again. But she still remembered the warmth she felt in the little trailer that looked like a tear drop tipped on its side.

Inside her kitchen she glanced at the clock, making certain there was plenty of time for the cookies. She got out her mixing bowl and started. The chocolate chips waited in their gold package.

Sandra came in at twenty past four with a story about how Mr. Aasen had to yell at the drummers for not squaring off their corners when they were marching on the street. She had one cookie and milk, so as not to spoil her supper.

Alex came home at quarter to six and showered. They talked a lot during supper and laughed even more. Alex had three cookies for his dessert and Sandra had two more to even it up.

Both of them thanked and hugged her, then headed for homework, so they could have an hour or so with friends.

After they had gone to bed, Maggie went to the bathroom and locked the door. After taking off her clothes, she looked at her back in the full-length mirror on the door. A latticework of small scars and two large red welts of scar tissue, the remnants of a beating M.F. (she did not dignify him as "father"; certainly not "Daddy") had given her with a razor strop. She felt the top of her head and found the lump, a reminder of M.F. smashing a wooden apple box into her skull.

It was a good thing Richard had never met M.F. The first time he had seen her scars and she explained them, he blew up and said he'd kill M.F. Not that that would be a bad thing, but it would put Richard in prison.

After the last beating, Hedy had finally kicked M.F. out. Maggie never saw him again, but he had contacted her three times.

The first time was a postcard from San Francisco with a picture of Chinatown. It read, "Happy birthday. Wish we could celebrate together. Love, Daddy." There was a mailing address added. She tore up the card.

The second time was a letter that arrived several years later. M.F.

was in the Cheyenne, Wyoming, jail and needed money for bail. He said he was going crazy. She tore up the letter.

The third time a letter with a return address in Sidney, Montana, didn't make it out of the envelope before she tore it into little pieces and tossed them into a waste basket in the Menninger post office.

Hedy packed and had supper. She wouldn't have time in the morning, so she bathed, set her alarm, and went to bed.

The alarm awakened her to a still-dark world. She got dressed, ate a quick breakfast, and washed the dishes.

On the front steps she locked the door, picked up her suitcase, and headed down Dakota. She looked back at her house. She hoped it would be there when she got back. It was truly her home, but she always remembered what Maggie had told her once, that what she remembered the most about the house was the smell of M.F.'s cigars and the fact that when he was around, no one ever laughed.

The white, two-story Great Northern depot and its platform were lit up. She passed the slough on her right, crossed a side track, and walked the steps to the platform. In the depot she bought her ticket and sat in the waiting room. She remembered when there was a separate one for ladies.

Other travelers came in. Some she recognized from her restaurant days as being from neighboring towns—Overton, Divide, Calvin City.

People began moving to the doorway. The horn of a diesel sounded to the east.

She didn't hurry. She had her ticket. She didn't care if she had a window seat or not—the trip would be mostly in the dark.

After people settled in, most of them dozed. The little villages that had sprouted along the tracks of the Carver Cut-off, but had never developed, passed silently by the windows, their lights as infrequent as fireflies, their life just as ephemeral.

She waited to get off in Minot. She had a hotel reservation. The station was brown brick with a green roof and a sign "MINOT" hanging from the eves. Each end of the building looked like Swiss chalets she'd seen in magazines. Some people were rushing to the taxi stand; she passed by, carrying her suitcase, and headed down the tracks.

It was early, but she could see she was walking on a path worn into the byproducts of a railroad: cinders, bits of coal, right-of-way ballast, an occasional rusted spike.

She walked under the Broadway viaduct, firmly grasping her suitcase, wary of some tramp jumping out and making a grab for it.

The mainline of the GN was on her left; there were small trees, shrubs, and fences to her right. She took the first street to her right and crossed some railroad tracks and the brick Soo Line depot. "MINOT" carved into a light-colored stone stared down at her. There were a couple banks on the corner, one with two Greek columns.

She saw a tall building a block up and to the left which she assumed was her hotel. She tried to recall what the reservation man had told her on the phone, but she wasn't good at remembering anymore.

She walked uphill and turned left at a building called the Kemper Block. As she walked, she could see that the tall building was the Clarence Hotel. She walked under a metal awning and into the lobby.

The desk manager was very nice, but he told her they hadn't expected her so early. It would be awhile before her room was ready. She asked if it would be all right to leave her suitcase. It was. She went out, found a small café, and ate breakfast. The coffee wasn't as strong as she liked.

In her room she rested, freshened up, and called a taxi. While she was waiting, memories of Maggie as a little girl covered with blood poured through her brain. The taxi took her to Broadway, then turned at the college, and went west to the Veterans' Hospital, an imposing building that was creamy-bright in the morning sun.

She told the man at the desk who she was and why she was there. He glanced at a sheet of paper, gave her a funny look, and asked her to follow him to a small room, where he left her.

A few minutes later he returned with a doctor, made introductions, and left.

The doctor pulled a chair closer. "Mrs. Vogler, it's an unpleasant duty that I have, but I must tell you your husband passed away not fifteen minutes ago."

Hedy was almost relieved. After seeing her daughter, bloody, ripped open, unconscious, she wasn't sure she could have faced Manfred.

The doctor gave his condolences, asked if he could do anything, and told her she could stay in the room as long as she wanted. He left. Just as the door shut, Hedy stood up. She'd been there long enough. She had a funeral to arrange.

The doctor and another man were speaking in the hall. As Hedy walked by, the doctor asked her to wait. The other man left and the doctor took her back into the little room.

"Mrs. Vogler, there's been a terrible mistake. Your husband was pronounced dead. His body was placed in an ambulance to be taken to a funeral home we use for indigents. Through a mix-up, we had no idea Manfred had any living relatives."

A strange sensation was creeping through Hedy's body.

"I don't know how it happened, but he came back to life in the ambulance. That's never happened before. I'm truly sorry. He's back in his room. You can see him any time."

Hedy was truly sorry, too. Everything had been put in place— the death, then the funeral, then the burial—now it was all jumbled again.

The apologetic doctor himself led her to Manfred's room. He explained that while there was a problem because of the way Manfred had been terminated from the Army during World War I, he wasn't certain he qualified for veteran's treatment, but he was so far gone with cancer that they had taken him in because they figured he wouldn't be there a week.

The thing in the bed did not look like Manfred, who had been burly, boisterous, a real fighter. Even covered by a white sheet, the thing was thin, unmoving, and except for the eyes, almost lifeless. The doctor told her if she wanted to talk to him, she'd need to close the hole with the flap. Manfred's arms were too weak to move. She didn't understand. He apologized again. She thanked him. He left.

As Hedy moved a chair near the bed, the glaring eyes followed her. She became aware of a sound like air whistling out of a small tunnel. The sheet near his neck would move in time with the whistling. She pulled the sheet down. There was the hole, a dark, empty circle in his throat. She saw a flap of skin hanging from the hole.

She had read of such things. Sometimes cancer patients could not breathe, so doctors cut into their wind pipe which allowed air in and out of the lungs, but which cut off air to the voice box.

A nurse came in, introduced herself, and asked Manfred if he needed anything. She placed the flap over the hole. A voice sounding like a wood rasp said, "No."

The nurse moved to the door and motioned Hedy over. After an apology, she told Hedy that the skin flap wasn't the normal way of closing the hole, but since Manfred wouldn't be there...She stopped in embarrassment. "Mrs. Vogler, I am terribly sorry."

"That's all right. I understand."

With sad eyes the nurse left and Hedy returned to her seat.

"Well, Manfred, I'm here." She put the flap in place.

"Damn time, too, Hedy. Vere's..." He rasped out the words and then ran out of breath. Hedy removed the flap. The whistle started. The flap went back. "Vere's Maggie? I vant her here."

"She's not coming, Manfred. You know why." She moved the flap.

"Dass kleine Teufel. She always was a Devil..." His eyes blazed and he was gasping. She opened his airway.

"Manfred, you almost killed her twice. Even so, she says she has forgiven you. She just can't forget." The flap moved into place.

"Forgives me. She cost me jobs, positions, a place as a chef..." Gasping was cut off by the flap. Then "Spare the rod and spoil the child..."

"You haven't changed at all. You are der Teufel yourself, not Maggie." Hedy saw that Manfred's face was red, so she released the flap and he was quiet while he sucked in air.

The flap back in place, Manfred rasped, "You always took her side. Now is no diff..." Hedy didn't move. Manfred's face turned pink, red, purple. Hedy wondered if she should wait for black, but then removed the flap. It took awhile for Manfred to recover.

"When I wrote her for money...to get my knives, my cooking utensils out of hock...she never answered me...iss dot gratitude?..."

For the next half hour, the two argued—Manfred in short bursts, Hedy in longer statements bathed in the memory of her failure to protect her daughter.

The nurse came in with some coffee for Hedy; it renewed her strength. Manfred slept. He did not move. If it hadn't been for the whistling, he appeared to have died.

When he woke up, they renewed their battle. Hedy had the upper hand; she could cut him off with the operation of the flap.

Their marriage; their children; his drinking; his inability to keep a job; her failures as a wife, a mother, a helpmate; his atheism; her need to have status in society—nothing was off limits. And nothing was resolved.

When she left, his fierce eyes followed her to the door. She turned and saw once again how small he had become. Neither of them smiled.

She called a taxi and had it stop at the small café. After her late dinner, she walked to the hotel and slept. She dreamed of Maggie in trouble, screaming, but it was dark and she couldn't find her daughter.

She ate supper at the small café, drank three cups of coffee. She sat in the hotel lobby and read newspapers and magazines until midnight. She went to bed and did not dream.

When she arrived at the Veterans' Hospital the next morning, the man at the desk called the doctor who had spoken to her the day before. They went to the small room where he told her that Manfred had died during the night. This time there was no mistake. He had verified the death himself. He gave her the name of the funeral home. She thanked him and called a taxi.

While they were waiting, the doctor gave her a small satchel. It contained Manfred's worldly goods.

The funeral director was very kind. He'd handled many indigent cases for the county and for the VA, so he was glad to get a paying customer—even though she wanted a barebones casket and ceremony.

At the funeral there were three people—Hedy and two bums who left when they found out there was no meal. No veterans showed up after they learned there was some question about Manfred's discharge.

When Hedy stepped into the passenger coach of the Empire Builder, she was glad she'd saved enough money to pay for all the bills that had emerged from Manfred's death. She slept and dreamed about her three kids when they were little.

After she rested at home, she called to have her milk and newspaper deliveries restarted. She did some house cleaning and baked a pan of chocolate chip cookies, half of which she put in a container.

It was a school day, so Alex and Sandra wouldn't be at Maggie's until later, but she wanted to talk with her daughter alone. She'd see her grandchildren if Maggie invited her to supper.

She walked up Dakota, carrying the cookies. She knocked on the door of the house on the corner across Stimson. Maggie answered.

"Mom, you're back. Come in."

"Here are some chocolate chip cookies."

"Umm, homemade. Stay to supper?"

"Certainly."

They laughed.

"Want some coffee?"

"Certainly."

They laughed again.

Sitting on the sofa, Hedy said, "He's dead."

"I thought so."

"And buried."

"In Minot?"

"Yes."

There was a long silence.

"My, this coffee is good. Nice and strong."

"Just the way we like it, Mom."

They laughed.

A CARNIVAL IN MY HEART

Joey Markesen was a worrier. Always was. Even in the cradle he had a worried look. In school he had no fingernails; they were all gnawed down. He worried about his grades, the weather, the news, the outcome of the book he was reading, but most of all he worried about his mother.

Joey was a posthumous child. His Dad, Joe, Sr., was killed on Guadalcanal by a Japanese sniper. His mother, Beverly Ann, was only eighteen. The wedding was what was called a "quickie."

Beverly Ann took the news of Joe's death badly. Her parents had to come out to California to help her through the pregnancy. Her mother stayed for a year because Beverly Ann verged on a breakdown.

Baby Joey was aware of his mother's emotional state, and that awareness kept him from smiling far beyond the time most babies would grin at the approach of a parent.

When her mother went back home, she sent a check each month to help financially. When Beverly Ann seemed to have her emotions under firm control, Joey began to thrive in his new environment. Then—disaster. Beverly Ann's parents were killed by a carbon monoxide leak in their furnace. Beverly Ann's emotions fell into a pit of despair. Joey went with them.

Beverly Ann had no choice but to move in with Joe's parents in their house in Pomona. It was not a good situation—they had opposed the marriage, thinking that their son was too young and had been trapped by the pregnancy which they blamed on Beverly Ann—but it was the only viable option.

For two years Joey listened to arguments, yelling, recriminations, and tears. He reacted accordingly; at one point the doctor thought he might be a victim of mental retardation.

Finally, Beverly Ann left with Joey, and a few months of wandering ended with her "shacking up" with a railroad man named Max, who worked on the big steam locomotives in the huge Illinois Central shops in Paducah, Kentucky. When Joey started school, he considered Max his father. His nervousness disappeared.

Beverly Ann got a job as a waitress at a café not too far from their apartment.

When Max had the night shift, Joey and his mother would listen to the radio, or she would have him sit beside her while she read the newspaper or the latest issue of *Popular Mechanics*, the only magazine Max subscribed to. Soon Joey knew a lot of big words. He was also fascinated about the way things worked, mechanical and electrical things.

The "family" had a car, pre-war vintage, but still it got them around. After the war was over and gasoline rationing ended, Max would take Beverly Ann and Joey for Sunday drives to picnics, local horse races and to carnivals. Joey liked the carnivals most of all—the luminous tubes and bulbs turning the nighttime midway into garish day; the brassy music, except the kind that came from in front of the stage where women strutted and shook with a lot of skin showing; the sounds of barkers inducing people to spend their money on games of chance, shooting targets, making a bell ring with a big hammer, seeing the wonders of a two-headed baby, the world's fattest lady, the world's smallest man, the only baby hippo in captivity, the Wild Man of Borneo, the Geek who bit heads off snakes; the smell of hamburgers and onions, hot dogs, French fried potatoes, caramel corn, popcorn, red hot peanuts; the taste of pink cotton candy and foamy root beer.

Just before the Bad Thing happened, they went to a carnival and met the family of another railroad man. There were three girls and a boy. Charley was in Joey's class at school and they played together at recess.

They saw an airplane ride. The girls were afraid to go on it, but the two boys climbed into the cockpits. As the ride started, the planes lifted until they were ten feet off the ground. Joey heard a loud staccato noise behind him. He turned and saw Charley in the next plane operating a toy machine gun. Sparks came out of the barrel, along with the noise that represented shots. Joey's machine gun was pointed forward, but there was a rear seat with a machine gun pointed at Charley.

Joey wasn't about to let Charley claim he shot Joey down and never got shot at all. He undid his safety belt and climbed into the back seat, where he began firing at Charley. Both boys were laughing, but there had been a scream from down below. When Beverly Ann saw Joey moving, she panicked. The ride operator saw where she was pointing and panicked, too. He brought the ride to a premature end.

Joey was upset that the ride had been cut short, but then Max and Beverly Ann caught hold of him and almost ran with him to the car. It was a quiet ride home.

Joey was sent to bed after his mother told him how dangerously he had behaved and how he had scared her almost to death. She left in tears.

While Joey was mentally retracing his actions, he kept remembering one thing—when he was up in the air at the carnival, he was never afraid, never nervous, not even when he undid his safety belt and climbed into the back seat. Then Max came in. He grabbed Joey, put him across his knee, and spanked him three times hard. Then he left without a word.

Things were never the same between him and Joey. His feelings against Max festered. Joey even stopped thinking of him as his father.

That would have happened anyway because of the Bad Thing.

After the war, the volume of railroad business slowed. Trains were idled. Men were laid off. Max became one of them.

Beverly Ann tried her best to help him; she'd check the papers daily for help wanted ads. Nothing she found suited Max; he wanted to go back to the railroad, the only type of work he had ever known. Arguments ensued. Max stayed away, preferring sitting in a bar to home. When he was drunk, the arguments were worse. Joey would lie in bed shivering as the abusive words penetrated the thin walls. Sometimes the landlady had to threaten to call the cops.

One night when Max hadn't come home, Beverly Ann let Joey stay up and listen to the radio with her. Sometimes in the late afternoon he would listen to adventure shows—*Challenge of the Yukon* with Sgt. Preston and his huskie Yukon King, *The Green Hornet* with its theme that sounded like a huge buzzing insect, *Straight Arrow* and *The Tom Mix Ralston Straight Shooters*—but that was the first time he got to stay up with his mother since Max had lost his job.

They listened to the *Lawrence Welk High Life Revue* and *The Longines Symphonette*, both music programs. He felt really good when his mother sang or hummed some of the songs. He fell asleep remembering her voice.

Something woke him…he listened. Voices on the other side of the door. Max. Loud. Threatening. His mother. Soft, at first, then louder. Both voices, angry. Joey pulled the covers over his head. The voices were still there, but muffled. Then his mother, begging Max not to do something. A thudding sound. A door slammed. Joey waited in the silence. Then closed his eyes and eventually slept.

It was dark when he woke up. His mother was still in bed. Joey spread some peanut butter on a slice of bread, poured himself a glass of milk, carefully so it didn't spill, and had breakfast. His mother was still in bed.

He opened her door and crept to the side of the bed. The covers were down and he saw she was still wearing her clothes.

The night light she always had on showed him how pretty she was. Then she turned slightly, and he saw the left side of her face was bulged out, purple, dark red, ugly. Her neck and throat were bruised, and he could see where fingers had embedded their pressure, dark patches against the white flesh.

Joey began to cry.

His mother turned away from him. "Joey." Her voice sounded like she had something stuck in her throat. "Can you get the big suitcase from under the bed and the smaller one in the closet?"

When he had them, she said, "Put them on the bed and open them."

After the "clicks" of the latches, he opened them. "Get your clothes and put them in the big one."

While he was gone, his mother got out of bed and began filling the big suitcase with her clothes. She put some of his in there, too, and the rest in the little case, along with some toilet articles. When she had finished, she said, "Joey, it's only five o'clock. Get some sleep. We have to leave today."

It took him a long time to fall asleep; he kept thinking how he should have run out of his room and protected his mother...

"Joey...Joey...it's time to leave. C'mon, Sweetie, get dressed. Eat some breakfast."

"I already did."

"When?"

"When I was up before."

"You'd better eat some more; it'll be a long day."

They hurried down the street, away from the brown apartment house, the railroad and the brown Ohio River behind them. The buildings were mostly brown brick. As he tried to keep up with his mother, he laughed to himself. Paducah was mostly brown; it was a brown town; that was funny, a brown town. Most of the buildings were two stories or had a false front that made them look like they had two stories. The narrow ones had two windows, and when Joey looked across the street at them, he thought they were watching him. He stopped laughing and felt scared.

He remembered his school was brown brick, too, and that he wouldn't see Charley again. His eyes watered up. But he scraped them dry with his sleeve.

When he, his mother, and Max listened to the Grand Ole Opry on the radio, one of the comedians was the Duke of Paducah. He was loud and didn't sound young, so Joey searched the sidewalks for an old man with a crown because kings and such wore them. He saw an old man, but he wore Big Mac coveralls, so he wasn't the Duke.

Finally, they came to the bus station. They waited in the dim light on a hard bench until the bus pulled in with a swoosh of brakes. As they walked to the open door, Joey saw a long dog painted on the side of the bus, looking as if it would jump over the front wheel. After the door closed, they settled in for a long ride westward. His mother let him sit by the window.

The bus crossed the brown Ohio and the even browner Mississippi. The bus left the crowded trees behind as it angled southwest on the sparsely treed flood plain, then west and through Miner, Sikeston (a stop), several small towns, Dexter (another stop), passing flat-land farms, Poplar Bluff (a stop), then chugging up the bluff and into the heavy tree growth again. Rolling land with hills overgrown with trees, rilled land with creeks and streams, the bus running on pavement that overlay the least-resistant contours as it followed the engineers' plans. The trees thinned out some as the bus raced the sun. At Springfield, they got out for a break and a quick meal.

Joey stood in front of the Greyhound Bus Depot and looked around. Next door was the St. Louis Street Coffee Shop and beyond that the Tinkle Bar. Further down a Chrysler-Plymouth sign and a Buick sign hung over the sidewalk. Much further down there was a multi-story building which may have been a hotel.

Across the street he saw an auto parts dealer, Dee's Liquor, a Texaco station, and the Hotel Moran. A tall building was beyond that. Joey began to count the floors, starting at the top, but his mother took his hand, and they went into the coffee shop before he had finished. He figured there must be at least ten stories.

His mother only had a bowl of tomato soup and the crackers that came with it. She ordered Joey a grilled cheese sandwich. They both had water.

They used the rest rooms, got on board, and the driver took St. Louis Street to the west. The bus wheels sang on the warming pavement, but the sun was winning the race. The trees thinned, the land flattened, and he went to sleep.

The bus passed through towns, stopped at a few, rolled down the Ozark Plateau, and entered Kansas. He was oblivious...

The bus station was on a street called Broadway in a city named Wichita, across from a multi-storied parking ramp. Up the street were the Skaer Hotel and a large cream-colored structure with "PETROLEUM BUILDING" on the side. They went into the waiting room. His mother had him sit while she fumbled in her purse for change and walked to the pay phone.

Joey looked around. The man behind the ticket counter was busy with some kind of paper. There was a large clock on the wall with a red second hand sweep. The walls were pale, but he couldn't tell if they were supposed to be light yellow, lighter brown, or maybe even dull white. The benches were brown wood and not comfortable at all. Then his mother was sitting beside him and he saw tears in her eyes.

"What's the matter, Mom?"

"Nothing. Gram's coming to get us."

Joey had never met his mother's grandmother. He wondered what she'd look like.

"I'm hungry."

"I know, honey, but I've used up our money. Just hold on and we'll eat at Gram's."

He held on, but it was tough. He watched the clock.

After while his mother got up suddenly and ran toward an old lady just coming in. They hugged for a long time, then walked over.

"Joey, this is your great grandmother."

"Hello, Joseph."

"He likes 'Joey'."

"Hello, Joey."

"I'm hungry."

"Joey!"

The old lady laughed. "Of course he is. You come along and I'll fix you somethin' to eat at the farm. All right?"

"All right."

She took him by the hand, and they walked outside to a brown 1937 Chevrolet, his mother following with the luggage. The hand was rougher than her mother's; it felt more like Max's and he wasn't sure he liked that. Joey sat in the front between the two women. He carefully watched how "Gram" pushed in a pedal with her left foot and shifted gears with her hand on a hard plastic knob on a long metal stem that came up from the floor. They pulled away from the curb, slowed through traffic, and sped up as the city fell behind.

Gram and his mother talked about grown-up things, but were careful not to say anything that would upset Joey; those things would be discussed quietly and later. Joey could see farmyard lights as they went by and the street lights of a small town they went through. Then darkness, a few farm lights, and then Gram was turning into a farmyard. She took Joey's hand and they walked onto the porch and into the house. His mother was close behind, but empty-handed since a man had grabbed the luggage and followed them in.

"Just leave those things by the door, Coop; we'll take care of 'em."

"All right, Emmie."

"Beverly Ann, this is one of my men. Coop, this is my great grandson Joey."

The man nodded at Beverly Ann and put out his hand to Joey, who took it and got a rough shake. "Glad ta know ya, son."

"Me, too." Joey was happy Coop never said anything about his mother's face.

After Coop left, Beverly Ann and Gram moved the luggage into a bedroom, and Gram made something to eat. It was simple food—ham sandwiches, potato salad, early peas, milk for Joey, coffee for his mother. And afterward a big slice of homemade apple pie.

Thus began the happiest time of Joey's young life.

Gram, Coop, and another man named Dick ran the farm. Coop was the nickname for John Haugen because "Yup" was a frequent answer he gave, and that was supposed to be like Gary Cooper, a movie star. Joey hadn't seen many movies, and he didn't know what Gary Cooper looked like, but if he resembled Coop, Joey knew he was O.K. Coop would show Joey how things worked, and when he had something apart in the shop, he'd call Joey in and teach him the parts and how they fit and what they did.

Dick Crenshaw was a talker, but did fine work. He, Coop, and Gram worked as a team. Joey soon found himself a member of the team—he had to gather the eggs every day in the small white henhouse. The Rhode Island Reds and the Plymouth Rocks produced brown eggs, while the Leghorns laid white eggs. At first he was afraid of the hens who were not very friendly towards him, but after he learned to avoid their pecks and the occasional beating of their wings, he began to enjoy his job and felt like he really belonged on the team.

After a time Gram showed him how to feed the chickens in their wire enclosure. He thought that the more he fed them, the less angry they'd be when he took their eggs, but it didn't seem to work out that way.

When he asked Gram why there were not "boy chickens," she said they could be pretty mean, and, besides, she didn't want any chicks; she bought those in town every spring.

During the cold months, he helped move the chickens into a corner of the barn where the heat of the cows and horses helped them through the winter.

His mother's face healed up, so it was beautiful again, but she liked to stay on the farm to help with the cooking, cleaning, and, in the fall, the canning. She never went into town by herself. She did go along when Gram made her visits to Grandpa in a Wichita nursing home. Joey went along a few times, but even though it was to see his great grandfather, he didn't like it.

Maybe Grandpa Rudy would be asleep. Then the three of them would sit in his darkened room and listen to him sputter and snore and not wake up the whole time they were there. Gram and his mother would kiss Grandpa on the forehead or cheek and then walk quietly out of the room. The women would shop, maybe they'd stop for an ice cream, and then they'd drive home past the ripening fields. Joey would hear Grandpa's puffing and blowing long after they left his room; he felt bad for Grandpa.

It was worse when Grandpa was awake. The head of the bed would be raised and Grandpa would be staring. He couldn't move, couldn't talk; the nurses thought he could see and hear. His eyes would burn into Joey when he came close to say "Hi, Grandpa." His eyes were the only things he could move, but it was more like a flutter. Gram and his mother would sit by the bed and talk to Grandpa like they would a normal person, while Joey sat in a chair by the door and listened. When it was time to leave, he'd go close and say "Goodbye, Grandpa," but there was no recognition. In his bed at night, Joey would pity Grandpa.

Coop bought some large firecrackers, sky rockets, pinwheels, and Roman Candles and he, Dick, and Joey had a grand old time on the Fourth. Max never let Joey have any fireworks.

When Gram drove in to church, Joey and his mother went along. Joey had never been to church before, and he thought Rev. Grayson talked too much when he got up behind his big wooden pulpit, but he liked Sunday School. His teacher Mrs. Starks brought candy every Sunday and handed it out when the lesson was over.

When Gram found out Joey had never been baptized, she got Rev. Grayson right on it. The minister tried to teach Joey what it meant to accept Jesus Christ as his personal Savior and to enjoy Eternal Life in Heaven. Joey wanted that because he wanted to see his Dad someday. When he asked Rev. Grayson if he thought his Dad was in Heaven, and the preacher said he did, Joey was sold: he accepted Jesus.

The next Sunday Joey was baptized in front of the whole congregation. Dick, who was a little more religious than Coop, was his sponsor. Rev. Grayson and his wife presented Joey with a New Testament and asked him to read it. He tried, but he had to have Gram and his mother explain some of the hard words.

Dick told Joey when he got older, he'd teach him to drive the tractor. It was green with yellow wheels and had an "M" near the front. On the sides it said "JOHN DEERE." Joey asked, "How much older?"

"Well, not this year...when your legs are long enough."

The harvest was just getting underway when the big yellow school bus pulled into the yard, and Joey had to climb aboard. He rode to town by himself even though there were a lot of seats and not that many kids. The school room looked a lot like his old one in Paducah, with all kinds of signs and pictures welcoming the students back to another year of studies.

One difference was the Readers. In his old school they had Dick and Jane, their baby sister Sally, Spot the dog, Puff the cat, Tim the teddy bear, and Mother and Father. In Kansas they used Readers with Alice and Jerry and their dog Jip. Alice and Jerry found more adventures out in nature than Dick and Jane did, and the illustrations were more detailed and interesting, but Joey didn't like the way they spoke—"See Jip. See Jip jump. Jip can jump."—any more than the simple ways Dick and Jane talked. No one he knew spoke like Dick and Jane or Alice and Jerry.

Eventually he found a friend, a red-haired farm boy larger than most of the members of the class. Joey and Harold Rains ate lunch together, tried to get on the same teams for recess games, and rode in the same seat on the bus.

One day an older boy, Donnie Durham, got mad because Joey wouldn't give up his playground swing. He grabbed Joey, pulled him off the swing, and threatened to "clean your clock." Suddenly, Donnie was on the ground, looked up, and scuttled away.

Harold put his arm around Joey. "Are ya O.K.?"

"Y-y-yeah. Thanks, Harold."

"Friends stick together, right?"

"Right." Joey realized he liked Harold better than he had ever like Charley.

The class got to dress up in costumes, masks, grease paint, or whatever they could afford, and parade through the high school classrooms on Halloween. They made Pilgrims and Indians and turkeys out of construction paper for Thanksgiving. They drew Christmas trees, all garishly decorated with poorly drawn lights and balls, and practiced for the grade school operetta.

Halloween didn't mean much to Joey; he had never gone out trick-or-treating, so he didn't miss not going. Instead, he listened to Gram's radio—*The Count of Monte Cristo* about a man who was falsely imprisoned, but escaped and looked for revenge; *The Baby Snooks Show* in which the main character was not a baby at all, but a mischievous little girl; *The Bob Hope Show* and both Gram and his mother came in to listen to the comedian; and *Fibber McGee and Molly* about a fairly levelheaded wife and her husband who was always having problems with the mayor or having to listen to the Old Timer, but Joey especially liked the voices of Wallace Wimple (Gram said he was henpecked, so Joey really liked him) and Teeny, who spoke in a voice like some of the girls in his class. He was kind of embarrassed the next day when he couldn't tell some of his classmates how much candy he had gotten.

Thanksgiving was different. Max enjoyed the holiday, but didn't want Beverly Ann to cook, which was nice for her, so they always ate at a restaurant, until he lost his job, then they stayed home and ate chicken. Gram bought a turkey raised on a farm a couple miles up the road. Coop brought it home and took it behind the barn, wings flapping. His mother made Joey stop watching out the window because she didn't want him to see Coop emerge with the dead bird. She and Gram made the turkey in the oven

A day ahead of time, Gram and his mother toasted thirty slices of bread and let them sit for twenty-four hours until they were hard. On Thanksgiving morning they let Joey get up on a stool and crush the bread with a rolling pin and put the crumbs in a large bowl. Gram melted some butter and stirred in some chopped onion and celery. After the vegetables were soft, she drained off the liquid. His mother beat some eggs and let Joey pour them and some chicken broth into the bowl with the bread crumbs. She mixed them while Joey added salt, pepper, garlic powder, rubbed sage, and thyme at Gram's direction. Gram scraped the mixture into a greased baking dish, pressed it, and put it in the oven until the top was crisp and brown.

Gram also baked some butter horns, while Joey and his mother set the table with the best china and silverware. Coop and Dick arrived, and everyone sat down for grace. Then the feast began. In addition to the turkey and dressing, there were mashed potatoes and gravy, buttered whole kernel corn, cranberries, pickles, green olives, carrot sticks, and cranberry juice in stemmed glasses with which everyone toasted a "Happy Thanksgiving." Pumpkin pie topped off the meal.

It was Joey's best Thanksgiving yet and while he liked everything on the table and the talk of the adults, he enjoyed the dressing the most because he had helped.

The men did the dishes while Gram and his mother went into Wichita, bringing Thanksgiving food to the nursing home. Joey stayed home and fell asleep on the couch, while Coop and Dick played gin rummy as quietly as they could. Coop carried Joey up to bed when the two women returned. He didn't dream.

Christmas was preceded by the operetta put on by the grade school students. The older kids got the long speaking parts, but some younger students were chosen to do more than blend into the background. Joey was one of them.

He was supposed to be a shepherd, which was what he was in the Sunday School Pageant also, and he had to recite a poem. He practiced with Gram and his mother until he had it perfect in his mind. He'd repeat it in his head in the school bus, during the "quiet time" in his classroom, and before he went to sleep in his own bed upstairs.

On the big evening the operetta went along with a few mistakes, easily overlooked by the adoring relatives of those who weren't perfect and by the other members of the audience because they were a small community and everyone knew everyone's kids.

Finally, it was Joey's turn. He heard his cue and stepped forward from the other shepherds gathered around some fake sheep. He looked at the audience…and his mind blanked. He couldn't remember the poem even though it was only sixteen lines long.

After a pause, it started to come. He began, "The sheep, the sheep." *What came next?* He couldn't remember. He repeated, "The sheep, the sheep." Still nothing. "The sheep, the sheep." His face was hot; his hair on fire. "The sheep, the sheep."

Then a miracle; the poem appeared in his mind. He became confident he had it. "The sheep, the sheep, so white and still; looked like snow upon the hill." He went on to the end with the sheep and the shepherds the first witnesses to the birth of the Savior. He melted back into his fellow shepherds.

On the way home Gram and his mother said they were so proud of him and the good job he had done. He wasn't sure how to take their praise because he had put ten sheep where there should have been two, and both women must have known that. He felt better when they had hot apple cider and cookies with Coop and Dick, both of whom said he would grow up to be a great actor. But they didn't know of the explosion of the sheep population.

Coop let Joey ride in the pickup when he went to get the Christmas tree. They stopped at the Standard Station where the trees were sold, and Coop let him pick out the one. It took him a couple tries because Coop said his first two choices were too small, but he had been comparing them with the smaller trees Max had put up in their apartment.

His big present was a Marx train set. Coop and Dick showed him how to set up the tracks, fitting the metal prongs from one piece into the holes in the next section and continuing until there was a setup with two curves. The yellow engine was a wind-up with a removable key; red and black paint marked-out the doors, windows, and other parts; the front grill was painted red. There were three cream-colored passenger cars with green roofs and undercarriages, with doors and a long line of windows painted orange. Near the top of each car was "UNION PACIFIC" and near the bottom "OMAHA" on two of them and "SQUAW BONNET" on one, the letters in orange paint. The box said it came all the way from New York City. Gram, his mother, Coop, and Dick had all chipped in to make it the greatest present he'd ever received.

Life was good on the farm. For nine months he had friends at school and during the summer he kept busy with his chores. He rode the big jackass bareback, exploring the shelterbelts and the far corners of the farm when he could get the mule to go, which wasn't all the time. He went fishing in a small creek although he never caught anything and tinkered in the shop with old engines; electrical devices that had quit working, including an old radio; and an ancient fanning mill. He tried to figure out how they worked or why they didn't work.

Sometimes in the winter Coop would bring out a wooden game board. On one side of the wood there were a checkerboard in the middle, some markings along each of the four sides, and four small green nets in holes at each of the rounded corners. There were also two small wooden cues. On the other side there were a slightly sunken round hole in the middle, surrounded by some "defensive" pegs, and three concentric circles painted on the board, making the hole the center of a bull's eye. There were also small wooden pieces called Crokinoles with holes in the center, so they looked like donuts.

Coop and Dick and Joey and either Gram or his mother could play different games on the board: checkers, carrom and billiards using the cues, and Crokinole by pinging a "donut" from the outermost circle, trying to get it to land in the target hole. Players had to try and hit their opponents' Crokinoles and knock them out of bounds. After everyone was done, scores were added up, depending on which circle the Crokinoles were in. The thing that Joey liked was that no matter who won or how close the score was, no one ever got mad or upset.

Coop had done some boxing and had some old gloves which he and Joey put on, and Coop taught him the basics of "the manly art of self-defense." Coop also told him bare-knuckle fighting was different than with gloves, so in bare-knuckle not to hit any place that was solid bone or he might break a bone of his own.

His mother got a part-time job at the five-and-dime in town and was able to buy a used Ford with good tires.

After a few years Joey's good times came to an end. The July weather had been hotter than usual and Gram had not been feeling well. One afternoon she went into her bedroom and didn't come out. When Beverly Ann checked on her, she was dead.

The poet Edna St. Vincent Millay wrote, "Childhood is the kingdom where nobody dies that matters." Joey's childhood came to its end.

The church windows were open at the funeral because there was no air conditioning. It was held in the morning before the day heated.

The preacher said nice things. Joey and his mother cried; Coop and Dick teared up. The burial was in the prairie-flat cemetery.

Joey and his mother went to the nursing home once a week for three weeks. Grandpa Rudy's eyes seemed to be searching the room. They looked right through Joey and kept going. Joey felt worse than ever. Then Grandpa died.

The heat was still in the church and on the prairie when Grandpa made his farewell and was placed in a hole in the Rudebaugh family plot. Joey handled the shovel himself when it was his turn to throw dirt onto the coffin. It was more dirt than he'd thrown into Gram's grave.

The Rudebaugh Estate was a mess. Gram owed a lot of money. As Dick said, "She was good at farming, but poor at business." After everything was settled, the farm was gone, Coop and Dick were moving on, and Joey and his mother were homeless.

They moved into an apartment that overlooked the business district of the small town. Joey was never late to school and his mother was never late to work. Mr. Blake, the owner of the five-and-dime, was so pleased with her work and was so upset by the way her life had fallen apart after Gram's death, that he put her on full time.

That worked for awhile, but his wife, who hadn't gotten over that she wasn't twenty-five anymore, suspected there was more to the hiring than her husband would admit. He put up with her accusations of a love affair until the next spring, but finally caved. He called Beverly Ann to his office, told her he had to make cutbacks, and gave her a month's severance.

She was stunned and it took her a few days to recover. When she did, she got a job as a waitress in the café just down the block. It was harder work than at the five-and-dime, but with tips she made more money. When Mr. Blake came in for coffee, he'd smile at her and leave a good tip.

That job lasted a year, but when it was reported to Mrs. Blake that her husband was smiling at the pretty waitress, her ire was aroused. She and her friends would go to the café just to make catty remarks to Beverly Ann and to complain about her to the owner. When that had no effect, they threatened to stop holding their monthly Homemakers' Club banquets in the café if the pretty waitress wasn't fired. In a small-town business, every dollar counts; Beverly Ann was terminated.

Worse, no one else would hire her.

After school ended, Beverly Ann and Joey packed up their belongings, and the Ford headed out of town. They passed through several small towns until there was a "Help Wanted" sign in the window of a restaurant. The old couple who ran the place were glad to hire Beverly Ann: two of their staff had just gone over to a new eating place closer to the highway. They even suggested where she could get an apartment.

Joey made friends with the grandson of the apartment house owner, so when school started, he didn't feel much like the new kid. He continued to stumble his way through the Testament, but neither he nor his mother went to church very often. She cried a lot in her bedroom, which made Joey feel miserable because he didn't know how to comfort her and, besides, her door was closed.

They were in that town almost two years; it took that long for the restaurant to shrivel and die. The other restaurant had a full staff so the northern trek began again. The little town they settled in had a creek, and Joey met a couple other boys his age fishing there. At first Lowell and Ed ignored him, but after the three met on the creekbank three consecutive days, they started talking and soon became friends. Ed even brought him an old bamboo pole to use.

His mother was waitressing again, glad that Joey had friends, and things went along well. Then Joey got in trouble. A widow lady had yelled at Ed for crossing her yard, so in revenge he talked Lowell and Joey into helping him rock out the windows of her garage. A neighbor lady saw them, the police were called, and the boys had to go to court.

Lowell, who had trouble sitting down, cried as his Dad glowered at him. Joey cried because his mother had cried when the police officer came to their apartment and informed her of what had happened. Ed and his mother scowled at the judge; the woman kept interrupting until he told her to stop her outbursts or he'd hold her in contempt. The sentence was that the families had to pay for the damage.

After his mother paid and they got home, Joey cried in her arms and told her how sorry he was. He vowed he'd never hurt her again. He also avoided Ed.

School came and went; he learned a little and was promoted. The year came and went, as did the holidays—nothing special; he longed for the old days on the farm.

A man bought the café. He was in his thirties, but had gone to seed, a former football hero at the local high school who'd married the head cheerleader. She was living in Minneapolis with their two children. He rarely saw them.

At first everything went smoothly. He seemed very pleased with Beverly Ann's work. Then she began to notice that when she was in the narrow space behind the counter and the malted milk mixer, he would need something at the end of the counter and would squeeze by, pushing his belly into her. Soon he began to stroke her bare arm when he was complimenting her about the way she knew waitressing. Then he'd give her a hug and say things like "great job" or "you're doin' great work, honey."

Beverly Ann was very uncomfortable, but she also needed the job. She began to avoid him in any confined place and tried never to be alone with him.

One night she had to close by herself. The cook had already gone and the other waitress had checked out early with a headache. Her boss came in, said he'd lock up, and went to the office, but as she cleaned up, she could see him watching her. She got her coat and purse, checked out on the time card, and headed for the door. Just as she opened it, a large hairy arm reached around her and slammed it shut.

She jerked on the door handle, but the arm held it tight. Then he spun her around and thrust his mouth on hers. His tongue went probing, but she kept her teeth locked. He pushed his body tight against her. His breath came in bursts and it stunk like an ancient armpit. They pushed and shoved each other. She was in better shape than he was and he began wheezing. He tried to grasp her head in both hands, but she ducked away and was free. He came at her and she swung her purse and hit him on the side of the head. He went down and she went out.

She cried on the way to the apartment, not because she was hurt, but because she was frustrated she was so small. When Joey asked why her eyes were red, she said the wind must have gotten to them. He knew that was a lie. There was no wind, but he couldn't think of anything to say.

The next day she went to the office of the police chief and told him what had happened. He was an old teammate of her boss and said she must be mistaken. When she insisted, he said making a false charge was just like perjury and she'd better think about it. Besides, hitting a man with a heavy purse could be construed as assault and battery. She'd better think about that, too.

By the time Joey got home from school, the Ford was all packed, and she told him they were leaving. She went a few blocks out of the way to avoid the café. They hit the highway and headed north. They didn't speak until they stopped to eat. As they ate, they didn't really say anything of importance.

Late that night, she pulled off the highway onto an approach and they slept in the car. They were awake before the sun and started north. No breakfast, a little dinner, kept going. They crossed into North Dakota; it began to rain. They kept going; Joey slept.

As they were coming down the hill into Kingston, something began making noise under the car. She kept going.

As they went up the overpass at Caseyville, the noise got worse. She kept going.

When they started up the overpass at Menninger, the noise stopped. So did the car. There was a burned smell. She began to cry. Joey put his arms around her and said, "Don't cry, Mom; we'll do fine." She cried harder and then said, "Yes; yes, we will."

The engine still ran; she had her lights on as they sat on the shoulder. Car whizzed by, some of them honking. Semis gushed water onto them. A red flashing light pulled up behind them, and a rain-slickered highway patrolman stood at her window.

"You can't park here, Ma'am."

"My car won't go."

"Try it."

She did. The clutch seemed like nothing.

He got down and looked under the car; he had her move over and pushed a pedal. "I think your clutch is burned out. Come with me and I'll get a tow truck. It's too dangerous for you to stay here."

It was Joey's first ride in a police car; he liked the leathery smell and the shotgun.

The patrol officer let them off on Chicago Street at a restaurant. "Ma's" was all the sign said. He brought them inside and introduced them to Ma, then he went for the tow. There wasn't much business and Ma took their order herself.

She was a tall woman, maybe six inches taller than Beverly Ann, with strong arms and a straight back. Her hair was jet black, thanks to her hairdresser. She had dark eyes and favored bright red lipstick. After Beverly Ann and Joey finished their sandwiches and French fries, she came over and invited herself to sit down.

Beverly Ann told her about life on the farm, Gram's death, and moving north. She didn't reveal anything about her jobs and the troubles they'd caused. Ma didn't say much, just listened and nodded sympathetically. When Beverly Ann finished her story about the clutch, Ma got up and went into the kitchen.

She came back with two pieces of banana cream pie and milk. "On the house."

"Oh, no, we couldn't."

Ma slid in beside Joey. "Eat." Joey dug in and soon his mother was eating, too.

When they finished, they both thanked her. "Think nothin' of it; I like to see people enjoy my cookin'." There was a silence, then, "You got money for the tow?"

Beverly Ann looked away. "Maybe. I think so if it's not too much."

"What about the repairs?'

Silence. Then, "Probably not."

"You got a place to stay?"

"No."

"Maybe you wanna work for me? I always need good help."

"I'm a good waitress."

"I don't doubt it, but I'll judge that later. I got an apartment upstairs at my place. You and your boy can stay there."

"But...."

"There's no 'but's' about it. I'd like the company."

The tow truck driver came in, took off his hat, and walked over. "Are you the lady with the Ford?"

"Yes."

"I dropped it off at the Ford dealer—he pointed vaguely to the north—you'll have to talk to them in the morning." He stood there.

"How much?"

"Well, it wasn't too far out of town—say, twenty-five dollars."

Beverly Ann looked down. Ma cleared her throat. The man looked at Ma.

"Uh, maybe twenty dollars will do it."

Ma's throat again.

"I tell ya what, make it fifteen."

Beverly Ann gave him a ten, a five, and a thank you. He left, with a last look at Ma.

The next day Ma and Beverly Ann went to the Ford dealer and arranged for repairs. Joey got to sleep late and lazed around the day, but the next day he went up the hill with his mother, and she registered him for school.

His classmates were mostly indifferent to him at first: they'd talk to him during school projects, field trips, and in the halls, but none of them became his friends. Then two things happened that made him a pariah.

The first thing happened because he wanted to make some money to help his mother. He noticed a high school boy at the side door of the Golden Crust Bakery early one Saturday morning after he had walked his mother to work. He and the baker filled an insulated push cart with freshly baked loaves of bread, and the boy shoved the cart on its two large bicycle wheels and little trailing wheel across Lamborn Avenue to a grocery store and unloaded some of the bread. Then he went down Chicago to other grocery stores and did the same until he disappeared at the corner.

Joey thought that if the kid ever retired, he could do that kind of work, so he told the baker he was willing to push the cart and to keep him in mind. The baker told the push-boy, who confronted Joey at school about trying to steal his job. Before Joey could explain, the kid's friends—all juniors and all bigger than Joey—began threatening and pushing him, so Joey shut up. The boy came from a large family and they needed the money. Joey was looked on as a "scab."

The second thing was because Joey didn't like bullies. Maybe Alvin Mills deserved it; he was a red-haired little wiseacre, and he'd smarted off too many times to too many older boys in his life, but he was only a fifth grader and probably should have been given a break. Jamie Bedard, a senior, was not going to give him one.

Joey saw Jamie grab Alvin and give him a couple slaps. After Jamie walked back to his friends, Joey went over to Alvin. "What's the problem?"

Alvin wiped his eyes. "Nothin'." He went over to the caraganas by the swings. Joey followed. "Ya need help?"

"Naw, he gets me just about every day."

"Why?"

Alvin hesitated, then said, "I called his old lady an ugly..." He looked around and whispered, "Bitch." He started to giggle.

"Why?"

"She sicced her dog on me when I was stealing strawberries from her garden. He ripped my pants."

"When was that?"

"In the summer."

"Isn't it time that Bedard left you alone?"

"He likes it too much. He's a big hero doin' it 'cause none of the older kids like me."

The Menninger School was a closed campus, so the doors were

locked during noon hour. The kids who ate there had to stay in, and the kids who went home had to remain outside until the warning bell.

A couple days went by and Joey had ambled onto the playgrounds after he returned from dinner. Most of the students were there on the north side of the building, but some senior high students gathered on the south side because they didn't want to mix with the grade school and junior high kids.

Joey saw Jamie grab Alvin over by the merry-go-round, slap his head a few times, and push him into the dirt. Alvin tried to get up and Bedard kicked him back down. Alvin rolled away and before Bedard could react, he was up and running around the building. Bedard hustled in pursuit. Joey broke into a run, also.

On the south side of the school, Joey saw Bedard sitting on top of Alvin, cuffing his head right and left. Alvin was crying hard. Joey shoulder-blocked Bedard to the ground. By the time they were up and facing each other, Alvin had taken off.

The two combatants were about the same size, but Joey had righteousness on his side. Jamie flung out a fist, but Joey ducked and it cracked into the top of his head, breaking a knuckle. Bedard cried out. Too bad. Punches to the stomach bent Bedard over; a knee to his head broke his nose and blood gushed; a kick in the groin put Bedard down. Before he left, Joey looked at Bedard and said, "No more... ever!" He kicked the ground and dirt spurted into Bedard's face. The bell rang. Joey headed up the steps to the door and the other students made a silent path.

Joey's class was General Science and that day they reported to the lab for an experiment. About fifteen minutes later a knock at the door and a message sent Joey to the Office.

He sat in a wooden chair until he was summoned in to see the Superintendent. Then he sat in another wooden chair while the man read through some papers. Finally, he looked up. "What went on during noon hour?"

"I beat up Bedard."

"O.K. Why?"

"I don't like bullies."

"Whom was he bullying?"

"A fifth-grader."

"Alvin Mills. Who appointed you Alvin's protector?"

"Nobody, but somebody had to do somethin'."

The man read through a note, rustling it a little. Then silence. Then, "You broke his nose. His eyeball is scratched from the dirt you kicked into it. Doesn't that mean anything to you?"

"Yeah, he won't pick on little kids anymore."

The man stared at Joey across the desk. "His folks are pretty powerful around this town. They want you expelled."

"That won't keep me from poundin' him if he keeps it up."

The stare got deeper; so did the silence. Finally, "Get out."

As Joey stood, he noticed that from the Superintendent's window, he could see where he'd laid out Bedard. He left, closing the door carefully.

He wasn't expelled, not even punished; none of the students could understand it, but they wouldn't forget what happened—Joey was ostracized.

Not that he cared that much. Ma put him on as a busboy and dishwasher, so he was busy after school, Saturdays, and Sundays until 2 o'clock. There was fishing in the Jacques River and a whole town to explore.

One Sunday afternoon Joey went walking north on Chicago. As he started down the street where it turned into gravel and headed into the river valley, he saw a series of trucks and trailers in a fenced-in lot to the west. There was also a large building with the sign "PERRYS' SHOWS—WORLD FAMOUS." The lettering also appeared on the white trucks and trailers in red outlined in gold. He kept wondering about what shows they were talking about, but the next week it snowed. Cold weather moved in for four months and, except for walking to school and back, he didn't get around very much.

In April he went down the NP tracks to see how it would be to fish off the railroad bridge. He spotted the lot with the white trucks and saw a man moving among them. He went down the embankment, crossed Chicago, came up to the fence, and said, "Hi."

"Mornin'. Lookin' for somethin'?"

"Naw, I just like your trucks."

"Swing over there and come through the gate." Joey entered the yard. "C'mon with me." The man headed for the large building. Inside there was a lot of noisy activity with a half dozen men working on trucks and motors. Metal-against-metal sounds, motor sounds, men's voices loud, often cursing, sometimes using a word that meant sex. Joey had heard the word before, but never in such profusion and never intertwined in such intricate varieties of phrases. He hoped his mother never visited the shop.

"We're gettin' ready for the season." Joey looked blank. "The carnival season."

"Oh."

"We route through South Dakota, Nebraska, Wyoming, Montana, and back home."

"Oh."

"It's time for the Big Carnival, not just the shows and midways; I'm talkin' about life itself. A carny sees life like nobody else. It's not all glamorous and romantic, leave that stuff to the poets and the movies. Once you see the Big Carnival, warts and all, you'll never want to do anything else."

Joey didn't know what to say.

"I've seen you at Ma's, cleanin' tables."

"Yeah."

"C'mon to the office." They went in where it was quieter once the door was closed. "Wanna pop?"

"Sure."

The man reached inside a small fridge. "Root beer?"

"Sure."

"Good, 'cause that's all I've got."

Joey relaxed, enjoying his drink, while the man asked him questions. He seemed very interested in Joey's explanations as to why he enjoyed mechanical and electrical things.

When they finished, the man asked, "Ever grind valves?"

"No, but I watched Coop do it."

"C'mon. I'll show you."

When they left the office, Joey wondered why the men's language had become so sanitary. A grey-haired woman came up to them. "James, I'm going uptown. Anything you need?"

"No, Addie…Addie, this is Joey. He's gonna do some work for us."

"Pleased to know you, Joey. Haven't I seen you in Ma's?"

"Yes, Ma'am. I work there. I'm pleased to know you, too."

The woman left the shop; the language resumed its male tenor. Mr. Perry and Joey walked to the back of the shop and stopped at an International. "The radiator's drained. Over there's the air filter, carburetor, and spark plugs. Over on that bench are the valve covers, head bolts, rocker arms, and cylinder heads." He lifted a heavy cloth and Joey saw an engine, or part of an engine, full of holes and dangling wires. He walked over to another bench. "Here's the valves." Joey saw metal valves poked through a small cardboard box in two rows. He picked one up.

The man showed him a circular hole. "That's a valve seat. Now watch." He smeared some moistened grinding compound around the valve seat and put the valve into the seat. He wet a suction cup on the end of a variable speed drill, placed it on the valve, and used a low speed to spin the valve right and left, up and down. After a few minutes he cleaned off the old grinding compound and added a new smear, then he started the grinding again. He did that a couple more times. "We like to do this every few years, so the surfaces don't get too pitted."

When the surfaces of the seat and the valve edge were shiny, he put a polishing compound on them and used the drill. When he was done, he had Joey work on the next valve, offering him pointers and little corrections. When Joey had done four, the man said, "I think we can use you. You've got a good touch. Think Ma'll let you skip out on some work?"

"I'll ask her."

Not only did Ma approve, she seemed pretty proud that Joey had gotten a job by himself. His mother was even prouder.

Joey ground valves, helped tear down engines, helped put them together, and did minor busy-work like changing oil and coolant; he learned a lot and then it was over. Just as school ended, the Perrys' Shows got ready to pull out.

Joey got up early and hustled in the dark down Chicago. It was chilly. The lot was alive. Engines were firing up. Lights were on. He saw Mr. Perry mount up to the cab of a truck pulling the ticket booth. It drove out the gate. Joey waved; Mr. Perry returned it. "Someday you can come along for the Big Carnival," he yelled.

Truck after truck went by. Tilt-a-Whirl. Octopus. Merry-Go-Round. Ferris Wheel. Bullet. Scrambler. Zipper. Bumper Cars. A half dozen little kids' rides. Fun House. Haunted House. Trailers with concession stands. A man jumped from the last truck, padlocked the gate, jumped back on. The truck hadn't even slowed. Joey watched the red lights climb the small hill, turn left and cross the tracks, then disappear. He walked home with his loneliness.

The summer passed with fishing in the Jacques and the railroad reservoir west of town and work at Ma's.

Ma was a big baseball fan. She usually had a Major League baseball game on the radio in her office and was especially pleased when it featured her team, the St. Louis Cardinals. Menninger had an independent team that played in the ballpark south of town. Ma would take Joey; his mother didn't care to go.

Ma had her favorite spot in the grandstand, close enough so she could jaw with the fans of the opponents. Some people came to the games just to hear Ma "rhubarbing," giving even better than she got. Joey had never heard a woman stand up to men the way she did; he was proud to be sitting next to Ma.

Ma also took Joey and his mother to the Dawn County Fair in Fishtown, where they had Ma's second favorite sport, horse racing. Ma bought some tickets for Joey and said he could go on some rides while they waited for the horses. As he headed for the Midway, Ma took Beverly Ann to the beer garden.

The game operators kept yelling at him to take a chance, but Mr. Perry had told him how fixed many of the games were.

He watched some hot-shot high school boys try their luck shooting basketballs. Mr. Perry said the balls were overinflated and that the baskets were not round, but oval, plus they were slightly smaller than regulation and higher than ten feet. When Joey looked closely, he saw it was true. He wandered off when the boys got tired of losing and left, followed by the operator trying to cajole them to try it one more time.

He saw a ring toss game with some twenty-dollar bills wrapped around wooden posts. Players would win whatever prize was attached to the posts they ringed—the twenties on a few of them, but mostly plastic whistles, Chinese finger traps, toy spiders, small plastic snakes, a little black comb, and stuff Mr. Perry said was "a bunch of cheap crap from Japan." Some of the kids were jumping and laughing when they won, but it was always for a cheap prize: the rings could only fit over the posts with the twenties from the back since the posts were slightly angled to the back.

A barker tried to entice him to play Bank-a-Ball, where a player bounced a ball off an angled board into a basket on the ground, but Joey just smiled and let two girls his age go ahead. The man said he'd show them how easy the game was. He picked up a ball and lobbed it underhand onto the board; it bounded up and settled neatly into the basket. One of the girls threw the ball onto the board; it missed the basket by three feet. Her friend's throw was even worse. The girls left and a boy took their place. He tried to put a little reverse spin on his throw; it didn't help. His friends laughed and they left. Joey did, too. He had noticed what Mr. Perry had told him: the operator was closer and threw softly underhand, so the rolling ball was more accurate, but the players couldn't go underhand because the edge of the booth was in their way.

Next was the milk bottle game—knock down all three wooden bottles and win a fabulous prize. Of course, it could be done. Try a free shot. The bottles were set up, one riding on top of two. The ball was thrown. "Wow! I got 'em." The bottles were restacked, but the top bottle was weighted and it was placed on the bottom and slightly to the rear. Money was put down, the ball was picked up and thrown. "Too bad, son, but you got two of 'em. Try again. I can feel your luck."

"O.K." More money was put down. Joey walked on—there's one born every minute.

Joey rode the Ferris Wheel and got a good look at the fairgrounds. He went in the Haunted House, which smelled funny, and smashed strangers in the Bumper Cars. Nothing looked as clean and well-kept as what had left with the Perrys.

He heard the Merry-Go-Round music and bought a ticket. As it spun, he watched the fairgoers on the Midway and the little kids, up-and-down on their painted ponies. The music, the laughter, the candy-colored lights even in the daytime, the people he didn't know. The expectation—he realized: *I have a carnival in my heart.*

He went back to the beer garden and waited, watching people; some seemed sad, but most were happy.

When the two women emerged, Ma was feeling pretty good. Beverly Ann had only drunk one beer.

Joey and the women walked to the grandstand. Ma had purchased reserved seating because it was right at the finish line. They looked at the black numbers stenciled on the white plank and found their seats. Ma sank down with a sigh; she felt good and there was no one in front of her.

That didn't last long. A large farmer in bibbed Big Mac overalls found his seat; a big blue bandana with white polka dots hung from a rear pocket. A broadbrimmed straw hat topped his head. He sat down and heaved out a breath; he was very drunk.

At first everything was all right, but then the horses paraded in front of the grandstand. The fat man stood up as he spotted a black filly. "Fleet Queen, that's my girl! Go! Go, Queenie!" The horses passed by and he sat down in front of an obviously perturbed Ma.

The first race started. As the field headed for home, the fat farmer stood up, yelling for Fleet Queen. As the horses crossed the finish line, everyone was standing, but Ma's vision was blocked by a straw hat, a big head, and broad shoulders. The man kept yelling for Fleet Queen, although she wasn't in that race.

"Shut up and sit down!"

Joey was shocked. Ma was mad. The man turned and almost fell down, but he sat.

In the second race Fleet Queen finished just out of the money, but Ma didn't see it because of the mountain of flesh in front of her. She grabbed a shoulder and pushed him down. "Your horse is done, so why don't you get out!"

"I'll go when I'm good and ready…and I'm not ready."

"Well, get ready."

Some people around them laughed and a few applauded. The farmer glared.

The third race was a photo-finish, but once again Ma didn't see it. The big man was on his feet, still cheering for the Queen. Ma knocked his hat off. It took him awhile to get it back on his head, but when he did, he reached over and grabbed Ma with both hands; she returned the favor, and the two struggled, trying to push the other one down. Both failed and gave up. Some of the men told the farmer to lay off. He sat down. Joey felt empty; his mother didn't know what to do and asked Ma if she wanted to go.

"Not on your life!"

The end of the fourth race brought the same blockage, but Ma had had enough. While the man was bellering for the Queen, Ma tapped his shoulder. When he turned, Ma shot a straight right, hitting his forehead with the heel of her hand. He went down, striking his head on the planking, and lay still.

A man slid over, checked on the unconscious farmer. "He's out cold." The people around yelled their support for Ma and a couple even clapped her on the back. Beverly Ann seemed uncomfortable; Joey was in heaven.

School took up, and although he wasn't exactly accepted, at least he was tolerated.

Perrys' Shows wheeled back into town, and he helped break down the equipment and make some minor repairs. He also spoke to Mr. Perry about joining up the next spring, but his answers were always non-committal.

Around New Year's, Joey became aware of a new rail who ate at Ma's.

He was in his thirties; medium build, but with strong looking arms; dark thinning hair he tried to keep in place with Wildroot; and a loud laugh that quickly got on Joey's nerves.

It was unusual for a rail to eat at Ma's. Since most of them stayed over in the Oleson House on Villard or the Menninger Arms on Lamborn, they would eat in restaurants on those streets. But the rail (Joey heard his name—Jerry Brickhouse) kept coming back to Ma's, sometimes with another rail, a small, dark man named Charlie, but mostly by himself.

At first Joey didn't think too much about Brickhouse. The rail would come in, order, shoot off his mouth a little more than most, eat, and leave. The next day he wouldn't be there; he was part of a crew that went to Fargo or Minot.

Joey was suffocating. School was boring, except for Shop classes. Work never varied—same old tables, same old dishes, same old customers. His room, if it could be called that, was so small, he felt trapped. When he was in bed, the slanted ceiling was so close to his head, it made him feel as though he were lying in a coffin.

When he heard the drops of autumn rain on the roof just inches above his head and listened as the water ran down the shingles into the gutter, he wished he could be a raindrop and glide from the house to the yard to the street to the river and begin an adventure, any kind, so long as it was away from Menninger.

Winter creaked along. Every bit of life slowed down. The one thing that made it tolerable was cute Sandra Fleming. Several times in Study Hall he had looked up from his work and saw dark-eyed Sandra staring at him. Quickly she looked away, her face all flushed. If he could be sure she was interested, but he could never convince himself that she was. Still…

When the spring thaw came, the snow banks on the south side of the streets were dingy white and still solid, but the ones on the north side were melting, and hidden bottles, cans, pieces of paper, cardboard, twigs, and last fall's leaves were exposed, leaving an ugly line of castoffs.

A change came over his mother, too. Little things—burning the toast, a stuck window, a worn-out sock—would set her off. Crying, yelling, lying in the silent dark, things Joey was not used to.

He began noticing Brickhouse flirting with his mother. Once when Joey was carrying a tub of dirty dishes, he saw Brickhouse leave a tip for his mother of folding money; most rails left a few coins.

One night when he and his mother worked together, he forgot his coat and went back to get it. When he returned to his mother, she was talking to Brickhouse on the sidewalk. When she saw him, she turned to the rail and said, "No, thank you; Joey will walk me home."

Brickhouse said, "Your loss," and turned on his heel.

The walk home was a quiet one, across the NP tracks, down St. Paul, past the huge Cunningham shops, and up Dunnell. By the time they reached Ma's, his mother was crying, but when he asked why, she wouldn't say.

The next time he worked with his mother, he noticed Brickhouse talking to her every time she passed with an order. If she wouldn't stop, he'd follow her along the counter to the kitchen. Finally, he saw her go to Ma's office. A little while later Ma came out and talked to Brickhouse, who left in a huff.

He didn't come back for a couple weeks. Joey noticed his mother was much happier. Then one evening Brickhouse came in for supper.

Joey was in the back, helping with the dishes, but if he stood off to the side of the sink, he could see Brickhouse, sitting on a stool and talking to his mother. She came back with the order, went out to another customer, and came back for a salad which she took to the rail.

As Joey watched, his mother turned away and Brickhouse reached out and pinched her bottom. His laughter followed her as she retreated to the kitchen, took off her apron, and went into the employees' bathroom.

Joey didn't know what to do. Maybe he should fight Brickhouse, although he was certain to lose. Maybe he should walk out with his mother when she took the rail's food to him. Maybe he shouldn't do anything. No, that was out.

He watched Ma go into the bathroom. He was sure Ma would make things all right. He went back to the dishes.

He heard the swinging doors, and when he looked up, Ma was cruising down the space behind the counter directly at Brickhouse. As she approached, Brickhouse said something. In an overhand curve Ma brought a big iron skillet down on his head, and he fell on the linoleum like a dead man. The customers stared, but did nothing.

Ma quickly went around the counter, grabbed Brickhouse by the legs, and dragged him toward the front door. A man jumped up from his table and opened it. Ma and her victim went out. She left him in the gutter, went back in, and retrieved the skillet. She told the dishwasher to do a good job on it and went up to her office.

Joey could hardly breathe. When his mother put on her apron and went back to work, he knew he didn't have to worry about her anymore.

Brickhouse must have put in for a transfer for he was never seen in Menninger again.

A couple days later Joey began helping the Perrys get ready to move out. When school ended, he spent some time writing a letter. He packed an old valise with a change of clothing, socks, and underwear; put his Testament on top; and hid everything in the back of his closet.

He pinned the letter on his pillowcase, picked up his valise, and crept quietly down the stairs and outside. He hurried down Dunnell and St. Paul, afraid he was too late, but when he crossed the tracks on Gregory, he saw all kinds of lights down the hill.

Mr. Perry showed him in which trailer to stow his gear. Then he took a flashlight and helped make final checks on the tires, vehicle lights, and hitches. His excitement kept building, and if Mr. Perry hadn't mounted the lead truck and yelled, "Move 'em out!" he was certain he would have exploded.

The dawn that appeared over the railroad tracks was cracking open the dark dome of night. The Perry vehicles were a line of cream and crimson lights strung out on the hill and on Gregory.

"C'mon, kid," the voice of Perry's oldest son W.D. called to him out of the semidarkness. The two of them walked to the gate. W.D. grabbed the padlock and chain and waited. Joey ran out to the open gate, put his foot on the lowest bar, and pushed off, riding the gate into position. W.D. snapped the hasp and headed for the last truck.

Joey looked at the line of lights on the street and followed W.D. His stomach tingled. A Merry-Go-Round started up in his chest. He was ready for the Big Carnival.

DOCTOR BEDARD MEETS
THE CHURCHES

D r. John Bedard met the woman who became his wife at the University of Minnesota, where he was enrolled in Pre-Med.

Violet Rice was from Racine, Wisconsin, the daughter of an executive with the Johnson Wax Company. Her mother was a woman high in the Racine pecking order. Violet was used to shopping in the best stores in Milwaukee and the even better ones in Chicago. The one thing she regretted growing up was the enthusiasm her father showed for the rather middle-class activities in the Wisconsin Dells. Violet went, but hated every minute.

Another thing she hated was having to listen to the *Fibber McGee and Molly Show* on the radio, just because it was sponsored by Johnson's Wax, so her father thought the family should show its loyalty. She thought the humor was low-class, almost burlesque, and she could hardly sit through the half hour, most of the time with the pain of a headache.

When she was introduced to John Bedard by one of her sorority sisters, she was attracted by his manners (almost upper class) as well as his looks (six-four, trim, thick hair that didn't give any indication he would go bald, dark brown eyes a movie star would envy). When she learned he was going to be a doctor, that sealed the deal.

Their wedding on the grounds of the Wind Point Light House was picture-perfect, with eight attendants apiece, the white buildings and the red roofs reflecting the bridal dress and red rose bouquet. Old-timers said it was the biggest social event in Racine since the John Dillinger gang robbed the American Bank & Trust on Main Street in 1933.

After a honeymoon in New York City with the couple enjoying Broadway shows (for his agreeing to go to *Our Town*, *Hamlet*, and *Abe Lincoln in Illinois*, she accompanied him to *Hellzapoppin'* (while he enjoyed the madcap slap-stick hodge-podge created by Ole Olsen and Chic Johnson, she could barely stay in her seat—the lowbrow humor was beneath her, and she vowed to improve her new husband's tastes). To that end, they went to the Metropolitan Opera.

A couple weeks back in Racine and then on to Minneapolis, where he was set to do his residency. Daddy's money paid for the honeymoon and for their apartment overlooking Hennepin Avenue.

Soon a little stranger was growing inside her; Daddy's money bought them a house to go with the Buick her parents gave them as a wedding present. John Bedard was an orphan, raised by a maiden aunt, who did instill in him some appreciation for higher culture, but she had died while he was an undergrad. She left him an estate of $200,000 and an appreciation he was not like the people who enjoyed hot dogs, working up a sweat, and driving a Chevy seven years old.

After their marriage, Violet elevated his cultural values and self-esteem even higher. There was an elite class to which they belonged through their breeding and cultural environment; then there was everyone else with their enthusiasm for baseball, Big Band music that was either saccharine-sweet or jazzy drivel, mindless movies, and books too horrid to describe—anything by Edna Ferber or Booth Tarkington, *Back Street* by Fannie Hurst, *Magnificent Obsession* by Lloyd C. Douglas, *Good-bye, Mr. Chips* and *Lost Horizon* by Hilton, *Drums Along the Mohawk* by Edmonds, and the worst of them all, Margaret Mitchell's *Gone With the Wind*. Both of them had read or had started to read those books. How could people put up with such pap!

They were ready to settle in among the Scandinavian elite of Minneapolis, especially when the hospital asked him to stay on.

A little girl joined them and Violet knew her family was complete. Her son Jamie wasn't so sure: he was so jealous, it took him three months even to acknowledge Melanie's presence.

Things weren't going too smoothly on the professional front, either. Other doctors, nurses, and hospital administrators noted Dr. Bedard's unhealthy attitude toward some of his patients. A word, a look, and the patients could tell what he thought of them; many never came back.

Called on the carpet, the doctor tried to defend himself, but the evidence was overwhelmingly against him. What looked like a promising career fizzled out, as did any chance of a practice in the Twin Cities, or any large hospital in Minnesota for that matter.

The Bedards moved north to Ely. They were there several years, which was surprising because they never fit in with the miners and lumberjacks of the Iron Range. The Germans, Slovenes, Finns, "Scandahoovians," and Poles worked hard and didn't have time for the aristocratic airs of the doctor and his wife. Plus, Jamie was an insufferable little brat.

The family might have stuck it out, spending as much time as possible in Duluth, the one spot of culture in the bleak northern wilderness. The trees seemed especially oppressive to Violet, and after one stormy winter when they were isolated in Ely much of the time, Violet demanded they move.

Dr. Bedard learned of a town in central North Dakota that was looking for a physician, so in the spring the family drove to Menninger. It was smaller than Ely, but the doctors were elderly; looking ahead, the town's leaders saw the necessity of new medical blood, so Dr. Bedard would be more than welcome.

In addition, there were plans for a clinic in which all the doctors would be partners, and Dr. Bedard would be an integral part.

The only pretense of culture in Menninger was the Athena Club, a group of mostly older ladies that met to discuss books and lend their support to the local library. However, sixty miles down the Gold Star Highway, Kingston had a college; and the University in Grand Forks and the Agricultural School, which was like a university, in Fargo, were within driving distance.

When Violet was introduced to some of the wives of the professional men and business owners and learned how many of them felt trapped in a waste of Middle American mental slush, she was sold. The Bedards moved to Menninger.

Not just to Menninger, but to the Hill in Menninger. The eastern edge of the town rose up the Hill, and the higher a family lived on the Hill, the more prestige it had. The Bedards bought a house, not at the top, but close. Violet made numerous trips to Fargo by car and one on the Great Northern's *Western Star* to buy the "just-right" furnishings she couldn't find in Menninger, although she did purchase some items locally so as not to alienate any potential allies.

And allies were what she needed. She enlisted them from the wives of the other doctors, the two dentists, the three lawyers, and some of the businessmen, but only the ones that had the potential to become "cultured."

There were several churches in town, but some were too small (Nazarene, Baptist, and a couple conservative Protestant ones on the west side of town); some lacked prestige and had too many farmers (German Lutheran, Methodist); one would never do (Catholic); that left the Norwegian Lutheran and the Congregational. After checking out the membership of each church, the Bedards chose the one with the most professional men, the Congregational.

The doctor and Violet realized they needed a base from which they could launch their campaign to improve the culture of Menninger. They quickly discovered it was not the Athena Club.

Several years before their arrival, the Athena Club members had gathered around a widow named Amy Peake, who was also intent on high culture. She played the harp and sang, the former fairly well, the latter could be disastrous. When she determined to put on a recital, the Athena Club members were thrilled and enlisted *en masse*.

It proved to be a disaster. Amy resigned from the Club and the members went back to their tepid middle-brow poetry, the latest gossip, and their first love, the Public Library.

No, the Athena Club would not be their base. The Bedards would have to create one. And create one they did.

Up until the advent of the Bedards, the most popular card games in Menninger were pinochle at some of the bars, whist among the ladies, and a high stakes poker game for the men after hours in Faxxon's Pontiac on Villard. The Bedards introduced bridge.

The Hilltoppers' Bridge Club met at least twice a month on a rotating basis among the homes of the members; sometimes it met more often, depending on whether or not some pressing cultural issue was at hand. The membership was limited to sixteen of the most-culturally attuned residents of Menninger, but four or eight guests could be invited to share in the evening's cards, lunch, and discussions. That way four, five, or six tables of bridge could be accommodated.

Once the Club got going, the Bedards brought up the Lyceum. The backers of the Lyceum were, unsurprisingly, the members of the Hilltoppers. They would organize three cultural events for the town in the late fall, mid-winter, and early spring. Even they recognized that high culture couldn't compete with good weather.

It must be said that they put their hearts into it. Some of the Lyceum numbers included the Minneapolis Symphony; dramas by Shakespeare, Chekhov, Ibsen, and O'Neill performed by the University of Minnesota Theater; a string-quartet from Winnipeg; both male and female opera singers; and *Swan Lake* by a ballet company from Chicago.

Of course, the expenses were tremendous, and the days of the Lyceum were probably numbered before the Bedards pulled up stakes and moved back to Racine.

The doctors, dentists, lawyers, and businessmen in the Bridge Club could only cover part of the costs, so their wives fanned out and requested many of the residents of Menninger to purchase season tickets. If that didn't work, they were cajoled or shamed until they complied.

Even though the seating in the school gymnasium or the Waterman Auditorium never was completely full for the Lyceum programs, largely because of a reluctant of the middle-brow men to attend, the Hilltoppers were thrilled by their success.

The Bedards felt they had succeeded in bringing culture to their adopted town. Everything was going along just the way they wanted, with a minor exception. Jamie was a thorn in the perfect rose of their status. He could be very belligerent, abrasive, and had the reputation of being a bully.

Things had come to a head when Jamie was beaten up by the horrid son of that common waitress who worked at Ma's Place on Chicago. Shrugging off all the pressure the Bedards and their supporters put on him, the school superintendent had the audacity to tell them he had seen the incident in question, and they were lucky he didn't suspend Jamie.

The Hilltoppers had neglected the School Board, so they had no real support from the farmers who made up the majority when they demanded that the superintendent be fired. They couldn't get their friends to boycott Ma's Place because none of them ate there. If they ate out in Menninger, the Club members went to the Menninger Café on Lamborn, run by the Nakamura family. At least the food was a cut above the regular fare in the other eating places, but when the Hilltoppers and others of the elite wanted to dine, they usually drove forty miles north to the Chuck Wagon just south of Sacred Water. Despite its unsophisticated name, the Chuck Wagon food was prepared by a trained chef, and it was the only place in central North Dakota that had lobster and King Crab on the menu and steaks shipped in specially from Nebraska.

Violet festered inside, thinking about her poor Jamie, terrorized by that Joey person. She gave parties for Jamie's teenage friends and made certain Jamie had plenty of money to spend on his friends and thus maintain what appeared to be popularity. Then Jamie graduated and went off to the University. Melanie was never a problem, and Violet loved how her classmates seemed to like her without any bribery. Life for the Bedards became idyllic.

Then Dr. Bedard met the Churches.

The Churches were a clannish group of four families on four

adjacent farms southwest of Menninger. The land was crummy: small lakes, ponds, sloughs, marshes, and a large gully pockmarked the land which was not friendly to grain crops. Horses, cattle, and pigs did well, as did a passel of kids.

Old Paw and Old Maw Church had come in a covered wagon from somewhere east just as the NP was building its branch line north of Kingston. They each homesteaded a quarter section of left-behind land, grubbed out a living, and bought additional land when their neighbors went bust. They also raised one boy, Lafcadio, who grew up as rough as the Church land.

He found a wife in a settlement west of Caseyville called the Encampment, a sanctuary for derelicts, outlaws, and ne'er-do-wells. They raised four sons—Leonard, Leopold, Leonidas, and Leonardo— and instilled in them a sense of self-reliance reinforced by an "us vs. them" mentality.

When Old Paw and Old Maw died, Lafcadio and his boys buried them on the "home place" hidden from the public. After a few years, rumors spread that the old folks were dead, but no official ever set foot on Church property to check them out. After the older generation in Menninger went to meet their Maker, people forgot there ever had been two old Churches.

Lafcadio and his sons worked in the dirt and dust; sometimes when they came to the town elevators with a wagonload of grain, they were so covered with grime, only their eyes and mouths seemed human. They worked with their animals so much that an aura of horse, cow, or pig afflicted any storekeeper with whom they came in contact.

Although they did shop at the general stores in Menninger, they didn't need blacksmiths, harness makers, or druggists—they made-do on the farm.

Each of the sons married and became fathers. When Lafcadio died, his body secretly joined those of his parents. The farm was divided into four and life went on.

As the little ones came, they did so without benefit of doctors or nurses, that is, until Leonidas' wife had a problem in the form of a breech-birth, a footling breech, to be exact. When two feet emerged from Mrs. Church, her sisters-in-law panicked. One of them even thought it was witchcraft. A call was hurriedly placed and the doctor on duty was dispatched. The doctor was John Bedard.

When he was ushered into the Church house, he almost gagged at the mess—scattered toys, clothing, tattered curtains, decrepit furniture, the smell of leftover food. But when he went around the corner into the dining area, he was shocked. Mrs. Church was naked from the waist down and was lying on a kitchen table with the leaves extended, her heavy breathing a heave that seemed to contract her whole body. Tears were on her cheeks, but she held in any real crying.

Dr. Bedard knew he had to act quickly to avoid brain damage, although he wasn't certain some of the Church children weren't already that way. He had water boiled, dropped in his forceps, and got to work. Luckily, the umbilical cord was not prolapsed, and since it was not the woman's first child, things developed smoothly.

After doing some sewing and checking the placenta, the doctor declined the hospitality of the house and roared out of the yard. No man ever appeared. In every childbirth on Church land, the men were absent in the fields or barns. Dust kicked up from the road as the doctor fled the scene; at home he got out the garden hose and washed his car.

Everything would have been all right, except for the Bridge Club.

The Club did not meet during the summer, but the Bedards did host a barbeque for the members. A week or so after the "Church affair," they had their backyard sprayed with DDT to kill the mosquitoes. A caterer from the Chuck Wagon set up long tables with salads, potatoes, vegetables, huge steaks, and marinated chicken breasts. The Club members would indicate to the caterer and his assistants which steak or breast they wanted and go back to their drinks and conversation. None of them grilled their own meat.

After everyone was finished and the caterer had brought forth the Baked Alaska from the kitchen, the conversation, well-lubricated with alcohol by now, turned to gossip and rumors. Dr. Early had just finished a story about a kid who lived near the river and had tried to use a dime to get something out from between two of his teeth; it got stuck and Early needed some pliers to get it loose.

Dr. Bedard knew he could top that one, so he told the story of going to the Church farm. He described the ghastly living conditions in the house and the appearance of the Church children in the same room with their mother or their aunt, depending, but his climax came when he said, "And there she was, almost naked, splayed out on the kitchen table like an old cow or a hairy sow, blood all over and two little feet sticking out. I almost threw up." The laughter showed that the guests appreciated they were not like the poor.

A couple weeks later school began; another couple weeks and it was the Bridge Club's first meeting.

During that time the doctor's story seeped through the town, but the further down the hill it went, the less it was appreciated. Out in the countryside the farmers and their wives didn't think it was funny at all. Eventually, it made it to the Church farms.

The Bridge Club members were making their opening bids when the front door blew open, shattered by the blast from a shotgun. Amidst the screams and cursing, Leonidas, Leonard, Leopold, and Leonardo, all dressed in their dirty farm clothes and reeking of soil and livestock, stomped into the living room. Some of the men, including Dr. Bedard, started to get up, that is until they saw the barrels of the 12-gauge shotguns brandished by Leopold and Leonardo and the five-tined pitchfork wielded by Leonard. They sank back, trying to look small. Many of the women were crying.

Leonidas wrenched Dr. Bedard out of his chair. He grabbed a fistful of hair and punched the doctor in the nose; blood flew onto the guests, the doctor, the wall, and the table. He punched him again and what was left of the nose slid off to one side. He kneed the doctor in the gut and the beautiful meal of salad, steak, potatoes, caramelized carrots, Baked Alaska, and Canadian Club Whisky spewed onto the table. "And I'm not payin' your damn bill!"

The Churches clomped out, Leonard's devil's fork guarding the rear.

Despite the encouragement of the others, Dr. Bedard did not report the incident.

A week later the Bedard house had a "For Sale" sign in the front yard; the family had retreated to Racine.

The Menninger upper crust had been broken. The Bridge Club was no more. The Athena Club once again defined culture in the small community. They added *The Life of the Party* by Bennett Cerf, *Blue Camellia* by Frances Parkinson Keyes, and *No Time for Sergeants* by Mac Hyman to the Library.

"ALL THAT GLITTERS…"

After what happened the previous year, Sheldon wasn't sure he even wanted to go to the prom. He hadn't been certain his junior year, either, and by the time he decided he wanted to, all the girls had been dated up. Then Claudia Steen walked into Home Room.

She was a honey-blonde with azure eyes, a self-assured smile, and an athletic build. Some of the boys immediately regretted the dates they'd made for the prom. Two days later Sheldon asked Claudia to the prom, and, to his amazement, she said yes.

It was even more amazing when she worked side-by-side with him when all the juniors got some time off from school to decorate the gymnasium. The crepe paper streamers; murals of tropical mountains, beaches, and palm trees; and what was meant to be "a little grass shack," but which looked more like a rundown haystack, were supposed to conjure thoughts of the South Pacific, which was that year's theme.

He learned she was a military brat: her father was in the U.S. Marines as a training officer specializing in self-defense techniques (he had even taught her how to defend herself), but had been transferred to San Diego from South Carolina. Because her grandfather who lived in Menninger was not doing too well and since her father wasn't too thrilled with the school she was in, he decided she should spend the last month of school in his hometown. She didn't care; she didn't like the school, either. What she did miss was swimming and body surfing in the Atlantic, but she could make up for that in the Pacific. Her passion was horses, and she had gone horseback riding with her Dad and Mom as often as possible. Her favorite color was Cobalt Blue ("Because of my eyes."); her favorite book was *Guadalcanal Diary* by Richard Tregaskis about the U.S. Marines on that South Pacific island in 1942; and her favorite food was steak, well-done and smothered in onions.

He omitted a lot of things about his life: how his father had deserted the family (the rumor was he'd run off with the milkman's wife who had disappeared at the same time, but that was just a rumor); how his mother rented rooms in their large house and required him and his two sisters to take jobs to help with expenses (his job as a stock and carry-out boy kept him from any extracurricular activities at school; his sisters had jobs as dishwashers and housekeepers at the hospital). Somehow he didn't mind working so much as he did the fact that his mother drank up some of the money from gin bottles she kept hidden under the kitchen sink—his sisters and he pretended not to know.

He did tell Claudia about his job and about the friendly rivalry the grocery stores had with their sales and their holiday specials. Baseball was his favorite sport; the Cardinals were his team and Red Schoendienst had been his favorite player until he was traded to the Braves; now it was Stan Musial; and blue was his favorite color (actually, he'd never even thought about favorite colors until she mentioned hers).

His mother was not too thrilled about his prom going because it would cost money for flowers, gas, and the traditional post-prom breakfast. Even when he said he'd pay the expenses, that didn't cool her down. He was already giving her half of what he made at the Harmony House of Food on Chicago, and she was afraid the money would come from her half.

Sheldon didn't know much about prom protocol, but he knew the boy bought the girl a corsage, provided the transportation, and paid for the breakfast. Male rumor said that a really appreciative girl would show it by not defending second base from exploring hands.

Getting to second base was usually easier if the young lady had been suitably plied with liquor.

To that end Sheldon stood in the shadow of the grain elevator on the corner of St. Paul and Dunnell and waited for "Highball Harry," a notorious drunk, but a reliable "bootlegger" for underage clients, to bring him a fifth of Seagram's 7 Whiskey from Helgo's Liquor Store. Harry came through, not getting drunk on the extra money Sheldon had given him and not stopping to engage old Pete Helgo in some endless and mindless conversation. Sheldon bought two bottles of Coke himself.

At the junior-senior banquet on Friday evening, Claudia and he did not sit together, so he had no real chance to talk to her. She was with two Steen cousins. He tried to figure out if they were first cousins, once removed, or second cousins, but gave it up as too complicated. She left with her cousins after giving him a smile and a little wave.

On Saturday evening when he stepped into Grandpa and Grandma Steen's living room, and Claudia came down the stairs, she looked like a vision in blue: eyes, dress, shoes, a purse that glittered blue in the light. And her hair turned her into an angel.

The grandparents took the obligatory pictures and promised him one. His mother never bothered to show up for the Grand March, but his sisters managed a few pictures until the spectators were shooed out the door.

The prom was all right, but so many guys wanted to dance with Claudia that he started feeling left out. She saw what was happening and turned down some boys, so Sheldon had more dances than he normally would have.

She knew of the post-prom breakfast and got extended curfew hours from her grandparents. After "Good Night, Ladies," they got into his mother's Belmont Blue Plymouth Cranbrook Belvedere (he opened the door for her), and they left with other promsters yelling "See ya for breakfast!"

Sheldon was nervous. He had the liquor; he had the Coke; he had the girl; but he didn't have the courage. He drove past the Burger

Baron…and Fries with its pastel neon telling everyone it was "Open All Nite." They kept going down Villard.

"Aren't we going to breakfast?"

"Yeah, but I want to show you something."

"O.K., but make it quick; I'm hungry."

He drove to Fifth Street West and turned south, trying to formulate a plan. Over the GN tracks, up a small knoll and past a farm, past another farm, and then a left, the night very black away from the town lights.

"What do you want to show me?"

"You'll see."

They were quiet until he turned off onto a little two-wheel trail and into some trees. They came out and there was the baseball park and football field. The road went around them and he started on it, going past the grandstand.

"I know you like baseball, but I've seen diamonds before. My parents and I even saw the Senators and Yankees play in Griffith Stadium."

"No, it's not that." He pulled off the road onto a path through the grass and into the trees. He passed several cars parked between trees until he found a spot.

"If you're trying to scare me, it won't work."

"No, it's not that. Just wait. I'll be right back." He went to the trunk, opened and shut it, came back, and slid onto the textured weave seat. He held up a bag and the two Cokes. "Look, whiskey and Coke."

"I don't drink. Now let's go. I'm hungry."

He searched his mind for something to say. It was empty. He put the drinks on the floor and looked at her. She had started the drive halfway between him and the door; he liked the fact that she wasn't a door-hugger. Now she had moved away and turned toward him. He could see the outline of her hair; he smelled her perfume.

It was now or never. He thrust himself at her, trying to get an arm around her shoulders, struggling in the dark to kiss her and blurting out, "I think I love you."

Claudia braced herself on the door and smashed her purse into the side of his head. He pushed himself backward, briefly wondering what the heck she had in there. As his head came up, she chopped his throat with the side of her hand; he couldn't breathe. Then a white explosion, followed by technicolor stars—she had driven the knuckles of her first two fingers into his eye socket.

She got out of the car; he fell on the seat. She opened the driver's door and shoved him out of the way. She tossed the bottles into the back seat and started the car. By the time they crossed the GN tracks and headed up Chicago Street, he could breathe a little. When she turned on Villard and stopped in front of the Burger Baron...and Fries, he was sitting up.

"You'll be all right; I didn't break anything, even though I could have. Come on in; I'll buy breakfast."

"I'll be in after while." The voice wasn't his voice, but he wasn't worried about that. He was blind in his left eye.

When other promgoers showed up, he scrunched down in the seat to avoid them. It wasn't long before he realized his eye was not going to get better. He started the car and backed out; Claudia could walk home—it was only three blocks.

On Sunday he refused to get out of bed. His mother yelled at him, but did not come into his bedroom. In the afternoon his sisters got worried and checked on him. They screamed when they saw his eye and nursed him with cold compresses. When he went to the bathroom, he saw himself in the mirror.

A few years before he had been in the Silver Dime Store on Chicago when he saw a hand puppet. He picked it up and there were two faces front and back on the head—one was Rocky Marciano; the other was "Jersey Joe" Walcott as they looked after their heavyweight championship fight, won by Marciano. Both of them had terrible looking eyes, all battered and closed. His eye fit right in.

His mother made him go to school, but he ditched and hid out in the rail yards west of town until dismissal time. When he walked into the Harmony House, the other carry-out boys, the checkers, the butcher, the produce manager, all had to look at his eye. Claudia had told her cousins and they had spread the news throughout the high school. When his boss Duke Hogan saw his eye, he could hardly stop laughing and told Sheldon not to come to work until it had healed.

That made his mother angry, and she wouldn't speak to him for a week, but that was better than the ribbing and the laughs he got at school.

Claudia and he never spoke again.

His senior year had its up's and down's, but he was passing all his classes and would graduate. For Christmas the family enjoyed a small tree and a few presents, but at least his mother wasn't drunk. She was on New Year's Eve and again on his eighteenth birthday. If his sisters hadn't baked him a cake and gotten him a new billfold, the day would have been unremarkable.

As his senior prom came closer, Sheldon mulled it over in his mind and decided for certain: he was not going to the prom again. Then Ruby Rae McGeoch walked up to him.

Ruby Rae went to the first eight grades in a country school southeast of Menninger (actually for her it was nine years because the teacher held her back in the sixth grade). When the MHS freshmen gathered in their Home Room on the first day of school, the new band teacher Mr. Aasen called the roll. When he came to Ruby Rae's name, he pronounced it "McGooch," which broke the students up since everyone in town knew the family said "McGawk."

Ruby Rae was neither the ugliest nor the prettiest of the girls in the class. She had reddish hair, a pale skin that took on a pink tone in the sunny months, light blue eyes, and a strong farmgirl body. She was also very buxom and that set her apart.

She was not shy. She came right up to Sheldon, who was just closing his locker, and said, "Sheldon, hi." He nodded. "I would like to ask you to go to the prom with me."

Panic time. After the debacle with Claudia, the prom was the last place he wanted to go, barring a vat of boiling oil, but he remembered a unit on manners and etiquette when he was a freshman. Miss Davis said that to be asked to a social event was an honor and that such an invitation should be accepted unless it was precluded by sickness or impending absence.

Sheldon couldn't conjure up an illness and since the family rarely left town, the absence excuse wouldn't work, so he fake-smiled and said yes.

If his mother had been unimpressed about his prom attendance the previous year, now she changed to livid. He could order his own corsage and he would not be driving her car. He thought not having a vehicle would break his date with Ruby Rae, but she said, "Don't you worry; I've got my own."

Ruby Rae had gone to her junior prom with a senior Dickie Davidson, who had a reputation, and not a good one. They never had made it to the post-prom breakfast. At school on Monday when his buddies asked Dickie how far he'd gotten on prom night, he just smiled.

After a couple days he wasn't smiling—Ruby Rae stuck to him like a bear cub on the trail of a honey tree. In the school hallways or whenever she was in town, she was always looking for Dickie.

The week after he graduated, he joined the Navy.

The boys in Sheldon's class were certain something beyond second base had happened, third base for sure, and a home run a distinct possibility. When they were in the locker room before and after Phy. Ed. class, they'd ask Sheldon if he was ready for a wild night (wink!), was he man enough? (wink!), could he go for a home run? (wink! wink!); they also commented on Ruby Rae's breast size and how lucky Sheldon could get after prom, second base being a foregone conclusion. The one bummer came from a boy who had grown up on the farm next to Ruby Rae's: he said he wouldn't touch anyone's milk jugs.

Waiting for the banquet in the basement of the Norwegian Lutheran Church, four groups formed: the junior girls, the junior boys, the senior girls, and the senior boys, based on their common interests. The girls were dressed up, but not in their formals; the boys were in the same suitcoats and blazers they would wear to the prom. When the door was opened, they walked down the basement where the tables had been decorated. Sheldon saw Ruby Rae grab a place card and exchange it with another one. When he sat down in his designated chair, Ruby Rae moved into the chair next to him and smiled. She did a lot of talking during the meal, but he didn't have much to say. In fact, he felt very uncomfortable.

On the sidewalk afterward, she told him to walk with her and she'd give him a ride home. They went down the Salem Street hill and came to her vehicle at the bottom. "STUDEBAKER" appeared on the tailgate, and it looked like a model from the late 40s or early 50s, but someone had been doing bodywork and painting, so it looked like a fire engine, a school bus, a lumber truck, and a gray whale had collided and gotten all jumbled up.

"Don't mind the paint. It's my truck, but my brothers are fixing it up."

Sheldon worked the next day, but had plenty of time to shower again before Ruby Rae pulled up in her pickup. If she thought it strange he didn't invite her in, she didn't mention it. His mother was passed out on the couch, snoring and drooling. His sister Margo was already at the prom (she hadn't invited her date in, either); his other sister Mary Jo would take pictures of the Grand March, so she was gone, too.

Once they entered the decorated gym—the theme was "Some Enchanted Evening"—Ruby Rae discarded the shawl she had over her shoulders and blazed forth in a bright red dress that made her really stand out since all the other girls were dressed in pastels. Around her neck she had a large gold necklace with dozens of rhinestones. Sheldon noticed that what made her doubly stand out were her breasts, which threatened to tear open the dress fabric. The other boys noticed, too, and the winks and smiles directed at Sheldon showed it.

Mary Jo took their picture as did Mrs. McGeoch, a bulky woman in a voluminous green dress. The Grand March went well and the visitors were told it was time to leave, which they did with the usual friendly griping.

The music began and Ruby Rae advanced toward Sheldon. He caught her in his arms and stopped her before her attributes smashed into his chest. As they danced, he held her at arm's length, wondering what to do. It seemed as though two living things were guarding the space between their bodies.

He danced with some of her friends from the country and was able to hold them close to his chest. Each time Ruby Rae came back to him, he was more willing to bring her closer, despite her dual guards. Toward the end of the evening, he could feel her breasts move against him as they danced.

At midnight the Principal thanked everyone and reminded them of the breakfast at the Burger Baron…and Fries. The juniors and seniors all applauded, the girls found their wraps, and a mass exodus took place.

As they walked toward the pickup, one of Sheldon's classmates yelled, "Take it easy, Shel!" but before he could answer, another one yelled, "Or any way you can get it!" Ruby Rae giggled.

Sheldon thought they would head around to Villard and go west to breakfast, but Ruby Rae shifted her way up the hill to the Gold Star Highway. They went north, then down into the Jacques River Valley, and then onto the East Highway. Ruby Rae kept up a steady chatter about how wonderful the prom had been and how lovely the night was. Sheldon didn't want to appear nervous, so he kept agreeing with her, but all the time was wondering where they were going.

After a couple miles she turned north onto a gravel road and a couple miles later turned into a grove where a tumble-down house stood—the Haunted House. Sheldon had never dared go there, even in the daytime, because a man had killed himself inside around the time of World War I, and people said his ghost still moaned around the place at night.

Ruby Rae stopped and turned off the motor. "There, no one will find us here."

"What are we gonna do?"

She giggled. "Wait here." She got out and climbed into the box. A cover slammed and she was back with a bag. She handed him two bottles of Coke and a church key. "Here, open 'em." By the time he had finished and tossed the caps out the window, she had poured something into two glasses. "Give me one." She poured some Coke into the glass. "Here." She poured Coke into the other glass. "That's Maw's glass, so don't bust it."

She started to drink, but stopped. "Wait. I'll make a toast. Here's to you and here's to me, if we should ever disagree, here's to me and nuts to you." She laughed and drank.

Sheldon had only tasted liquor once. He had found one of his mother's gin bottles in the trash with just a hint of gin left. On a dare he made to himself, he lifted it and let some gin fall on his tongue. It burned and he wondered why people drank.

"C'mon, drink up. There's more left."

He drank and it wasn't bad, more bite than a normal Coke, but not bad. He drank again. She finished hers. "Drink up." He did. She took his glass and placed it beside hers on the floor. "C'mere." She reached an arm around him, pulled him over, and kissed him. Her other arm went around him, followed by another kiss. He began to enjoy himself.

She went back to the glasses and the mixing. "I got the good stuff, some Harper's." She handed him a glass and drank from hers. They nursed a couple drinks in silence, then she took his glass and they kissed.

Suddenly, he felt her tongue in his mouth. At first, he was disgusted, but then he wasn't. He'd heard about French kissing, of course, but he'd imagined it would be slimy. Instead, it was smooth and exciting. He dared himself and put his tongue into her mouth. She arched her back and their tongues darted and thrusted.

She tried to get closer to him, but she kicked over the glasses. The gear shift was on the floor and was a long, thin barrier. "C'mon." She opened her door and got out. He hesitated, but followed. She was already in the box, throwing blankets and two pillows out of a large chest. "These belong to Maw so don't get 'em dirty."

She spread out a blanket and put the pillows down. She placed her head on one and opened her arms. "C'mere." If he was going to run, that was the time. Instead, he lay beside her and they began kissing.

After they had broken apart and reformed in more kisses several times, she said, "Shel, go get the fixin's."

He got the whiskey and the bag which contained several more Cokes. She mixed, they drank; they kissed.

Eventually, his hands began creeping along. She didn't stop him. He was partly on top of her and his hands rested on her breasts. She pushed him off and he thought he had gone too far. He was about to apologize when she began undoing the top of her dress and unhooking her rather extensive bra. She lay back and actually put his hands back in their former position. Almost involuntarily they began to feel and press and cuddle and hold and lightly squeeze.

When his grandmother was still alive, he had walked to her house when he was about five. She was in the kitchen and talked with him while she worked. She had put some flour on a flat piece of wood and had just placed a large ball of dough on the wood when he came calling. He watched her as she worked the dough with her hands and fingers. When he asked what she was doing, she said she was kneading the dough.

As he worked his hands around Ruby Rae's chest, he began to laugh. He was kneading her breasts. When she asked what was so funny, he told her and she joined in the laughter. They were feeling pretty good, thanks to the liquor. They stopped to have some more.

When they finished, things got more serious and after fifteen minutes they were both naked, writhing around like two mating cobras, sometimes he was on top, sometimes she was.

Things began to cloud his brain. Where was he? Oh, yeah, with Ruby Rae. Was it night? It must be; there's a full moon. Where were his clothes? He didn't know.

Ruby Rae was top of him, moving her hips. Whatever was happening down there felt wonderfully exciting. He looked up and he saw two large moons, each with a dark spot in the middle, moving up and down, with a glittering sparkle of rhinestones above them. Then everything went black.

When he regained a little consciousness, Ruby Rae was struggling to pull up his pants. "Shel, thank goodness you're awake. Help me."

In a faded dream world he helped her. He was even able to get into the cab with a little help. As she started the Studebaker, he noticed it was beginning to get light. The next thing he knew, two men were carrying him into a strange house.

A male voice said, "What's wrong, boy? Can't hold your liquor?" Rough hands stripped him and held him under an icy shower. It made him cold; it did not make him sober. He was toweled, dressed, and placed in a vehicle. He slept.

When they bounded over a bump and across a bridge on the Jacques, he opened his eyes. Mr. McGeoch was driving; Ruby Rae's four brothers were squeezed into the seats. He went back to sleep; his head hurt.

The car stopped. He was taken out and helped up the steps to the front door. "Can you make it?"

"Yeah." He grabbed the door handle. The men left. He went inside. He shut the door and leaned against the wall. He made his way to the stairs. The room seemed to spin. He got down on all fours and crawled up the stairs. At the top he stood up and worked his way down the hall, past Mr. Parkins' room, past Mr. Anderson's room, where a radio was playing softly. His room was at the end of the hall. He fell onto the bed fully clothed and slept.

When he woke up, it was afternoon. He inched his way downstairs, trying not to move his head. His mother was on the couch, an ice bag on her head. "What time d'ya git in?" He didn't know. "Never mind. I don't care."

He went to the kitchen, soaked a cloth in cold water, and made a compress for his aching head. He went back to the living room and sat in the big chair. He put the compress on his forehead. His mother was asleep. Soon, so was he.

On Monday he felt better and went to school. He was at his locker when the bus came in with Ruby Rae. He saw her walking down the hall toward him. She was wearing her corsage. He couldn't understand it: he had tossed his boutonniere when he put away his suit coat, just like he had tossed the one Claudia had given him.

"Good morning, honey."

"Uh, morning."

"Ready? Let's go to Home Room." Her arm entwined his. They stopped at her locker and went on together. When they sat down in adjoining desks, the boys that came in gave him knowing looks and sly smiles. Ruby Rae talked; he listened, but didn't hear much of what she said. He was wondering how he'd gotten into such a big mess.

Suddenly she stood up. "Oh, I forgot something." She hurried out. Sheldon looked over at Bill Mitchell, hoping to catch his eye so they could talk baseball. Ruby Rae came back, happy she had made it before roll was taken. She held out a necktie. "Here, Sheldon, you forgot your tie in the pickup."

Sheldon took it as everyone within earshot of Ruby Rae burst out in laughter. Sheldon turned almost as red as Ruby Rae's prom dress. He breathed again when Coach Chase came in, told everyone to quiet down, and began the roll call.

For the rest of the school year, he couldn't shake Ruby Rae. She was always close to him in school and a couple times a week would be in the Harmony House, sometimes with her mother to shop, but often just to smile at him or try to talk, even though she could see he was busy.

What was worse was her father and her brothers in the store, staring at him. He remembered prom night. What had they done? Had they gone all the way? Was she pregnant? Would he have to get married?

He tried to devise a way to ask her, but it all came down to "Ruby Rae, did we have sex?" That was something he could never ask her. As he understood it, sex was supposed to be a pleasurable explosion, remembered forever. How could he reveal he didn't remember: she'd be crushed.

She asked him out a couple times, but he always said he had to work or his mother needed him for something. When graduation came, she invited him to her reception and said she'd even pick him up. He lied and said his mother was holding a reception for him, so he couldn't make it. Actually, a reception had never dawned on his mother, and after the family returned from the ceremony, he went up to bed.

His mother was glad he'd graduated: now he could work more hours at the store. Ruby Rae was glad, too, because she had plans.

One Saturday night she parked her pickup by the Ford dealer on Lamborn and waited for Sheldon to get off work. Once he started walking toward home, she pulled up beside him and offered him a ride. Sheldon was trapped.

She stopped in front of his house and said she wanted to talk. She did almost all the talking. She loved him and wanted to get married. He almost asked about a pregnancy, but chickened out. She asked if he loved her. When he hesitated, she broke down in tears. To get her to stop crying, he said, "I love you."

She wrapped him in her arms and kissed him so hard his lips were hurting. She asked when they could get married. When he hesitated, the tears flowed again and she began wailing. Afraid his mother would hear, he told her any time she wanted. There were more kisses, hugs, and when she said she loved him, he was afraid not to, so he said he loved her, too.

She started the pickup and he got out. She said she was going to tell her parents the good news. He started to tell her not to, but remembered the wailing and went in to bed.

On Monday Ruby Rae and her whole family trooped into the Harmony House. The men just stood there, staring at him, but Mrs. McGeoch took his hands in hers, called him "son," and whispered he'd have to come to the farm so they could make plans. Ruby Rae was beaming.

After the clan had trooped out, Duke and some of the employees kept bugging him about what was going on, but he clammed up and said they wanted him to start coming to their church. Since the McGeochs rarely attended church, no one believed him.

The next day he went to the lobby of the Menninger Arms and talked to the clerk. That night he packed a large suitcase and after midnight stashed it behind a spirea bush. After supper the next night, he told his mother he was going uptown to meet Bill Mitchell. He rescued the suitcase and headed uptown via the alleys.

He came out at the Menninger Arms and walked into the lobby. He sat behind a potted palm, hoping no one would see him. The minute hand on the large clock ticked its slow pace. He put the suitcase behind his chair. If someone saw him with it, they might figure out what he was doing and tell his mother. When she found out he'd stolen her suitcase, she'd have him arrested. The clock seemed frozen.

Three men got up and he saw a silver flash outside on Lamborn. One of them opened the door and he heard air brakes. He let the men board the bus, then he made a dash for it, holding out the ticket he had purchased earlier to the driver. He put the suitcase with the other luggage. The driver stowed it, looked around for any stragglers, and got in his seat. He checked one more time and closed the door. The bus pulled away.

Sheldon watched the streets and buildings go by. Soon they were going up the hill to the Gold Star Highway. They turned south and went up and down the overpass. They went into a long left-hand curve. The town lights were gone.

They turned into a right-hand curve and up a little rise onto flat land.

Sheldon looked out. There was a dark shelterbelt and above it the stars were glittering like he'd never seen.

GOD WILL PROVIDE

D enny and Lenny Hoge were holy terrors. Anyone in Menninger would agree to that. From disrupting school plays with their antics, breaking windows in abandoned buildings and suspected of doing the same to a few occupied ones, to rolling a used grain auger from behind the J.I. Case dealership to the corner of Lamborn and Dakota, emptying the gas tank onto the pavement and lighting the liquid on fire. When Chief Coulson asked them why, the twins said it was their birthday.

At first, they would spend the summers with their grandparents in town while Tom and Virginia Hoge got a rest out on their farm. Then the grandparents moved to Fargo and Tom lost the farm; he was an average farmer, but a terrible money manager.

Tom tried to protect his boys from the law as much as he could, promising better behavior and persuading the judge to issue fines or community work, not reform school, but the pressure got to be too much for him, so he wasn't around when the twins concocted their greatest coup.

On Halloween night in 1956, the twins got on top of the Menninger School. They had rigged up a rope harness, Lenny got into it, and Denny lowered him down the side of the building to where "MENNINGER PUBLIC SCHOOL" was painted. Lenny used white paint to blot out the "L" in the middle word. What was even better was they got away with it. Despite rumors, nothing was ever proven that would stand up in a court of law.

Tom had begun working on the Great Northern between Fargo, Menninger, and Minot, where he laid over. After meeting Sally Ellington at the Four Deuces bar, "laying over" became even more physical. She had a white frame house on a street where North Hill started to elevate out of the Souris River Valley. She was a middle-aged widow, still kind of cute, and her house was quiet, unlike the house he shared with his family in Menninger.

She also had a wild streak that emerged when she was drunk. The married GN crew members had formed a Key Club. A couple times a month, they'd meet in a bar, hoist a few, and then toss their house keys into a hat. Each one would pick out a key and go to the number of the house on it. The rule was no one could stay past two A.M.—the Club was for sex, not anything more, such as romance or love.

When Sally heard about the Club, she wanted in. Tom had not been eligible since his wife wasn't in Minot, but when the Club members saw Sally, they said Tom could join. At first, it was exciting—different houses, different women, not all of them attractive, but being with them in bed stirred his blood and made him feel a lot younger than he was.

After a year, his enthusiasm began to drain away, even though new women were brought in when their husbands transferred to Minot. When he climbed into bed with Sally, she was usually drunk and snoring and the sheets were soiled, so he'd climb out and sleep on the couch. He and Virginia had already divorced, and he didn't want to go back to Menninger and the pressures there anyway. He transferred to the West Coast and his wife and sons disappeared from his life.

When the divorce was finalized, Virginia sat down with her sons and quoted Scripture. Philippians 4:19 "And my God will provide every need of yours according to his riches in glory in Christ Jesus." Virginia had dug out her old Bible after she was notified that Tom was seeking a divorce. Reading it became a comfort for her and she hoped it would be for the twins, too. "Remember, boys, God will provide." At first, her Bible was enough.

The sense of abandonment the twins felt with the absence of their father was smoothed over by their mother's simple faith, and a love for her grew they'd never had before.

Though Denny and Lenny didn't take up Bible reading, they actually settled down after graduation. In Denny's case, he had to—he'd signed up for a two-year hitch in the Army. Lenny went to work for Ambrose Harrington, a farmer whose spread lay north of Menninger along the NP tracks and extending west following the line of glacial hills. Harrington had become less diversified as the years went by, cutting down on the grain and the cattle. Instead, he turned to pigs. Hundreds of them. His nickname became "Hogger" Harrington. Lenny helped take care of the pigs. He didn't mind it; the pay was good and if the pigs with symptoms of diseases like coccidiosis and swine dysentery, respiratory and skin diseases, and parasites were culled in time, raising pigs wasn't that bad.

Well, part of it was bad—castrating the young pigs. Mr. Harrington told him it was necessary because the castrated pigs, which he called barrows, made good pork, but any pig that grew into a boar made meat with a "boar odor" and people wouldn't buy it. Mr. Harrington showed him how castration was done and Lenny got used to it, everything, that is, except the frantic squeals of the piglet involved.

Lenny moved to a little house on the Harrington place, and Denny was with the Army in West Germany. Virginia rattled around the house she had gotten through the divorce settlement. Even though Lenny stopped in a couple times a week and always took her out to Sunday dinner, she realized the emotion, if it was an emotion, she felt most often was loneliness. After while the Bible wasn't enough. She started going to the bars. Her solace became the Bible and the Bottle.

She didn't go to drink, just to talk to people and nurse a beer. Then she met Bert Hamilton. He was a mechanic at Menninger Motors, the Chevy-Olds and J.I Case dealer. He rented an apartment on the second floor of the telephone building across the street from where he worked. It was only a couple blocks from Virginia's house, but she had never seen him until he offered to buy her a drink at the Captain's Quarters.

They played some darts with another couple and did a lot of laughing. When he walked her home, he didn't kiss her and she took that as a compliment. After all, she was what they called "a nice girl."

As time went on, she became less and less nice. She invited him in, and they enjoyed themselves in bed, although it was a little less than satisfying since they were both drunk. Eventually, he left his apartment and moved in with her.

Lenny didn't approve and spent less time with his mother. He wrote to Denny, who didn't approve, either.

Virginia got a small alimony payment from Tom (when he bothered to pay it), the twins gave her some money every month, and she got a job as a part-time saleslady at Davenport's Department Store. Bert bought some food and complained if she asked for anything more.

When a storm blew in and tore down a large cottonwood limb that put a hole in her roof, she couldn't pay for the repair. When Lenny saw the hole covered with a tarp, he asked what she intended to do about it. She opened her Bible to Psalm 18:2 "The Lord is my rock and my fortress and my deliverer, my God, my rock, in whom I take refuge, my shield, and the horn of my salvation, my stronghold." She hugged Lenny and said, "Remember, son, God will provide."

Between them, Denny and Lenny had her roof repaired. She never asked the carpenters who was paying them; she just thanked the Lord.

When Denny came back from the Army, he got a job in Caseyville, sixteen miles south of Menninger, in an elevator beside the Soo Line tracks that had two storage units that looked like conical metal tents. It wasn't long and he was engaged to the office secretary Susie Charles. On Sundays they went for drives in his new Pontiac, sometimes to Menninger. Virginia liked Susie and looked forward to their wedding.

One afternoon Lenny came into town to pick up some feed. He stopped at Davenport's, but Ruth, the maiden sister of the owner, told him that Virginia had called in sick the previous three days.

He drove down Chicago Street and stopped in front of the

Menninger Feed and Seed. As his old classmate Slats Gregory helped him put the sacks in the pickup box, he asked, "How's your Mom?"

"Why, what's wrong?"

Slats looked around as though he were guilty of something. "Well, Saturday night I stopped in the Royal Flush for a brew, and your Mom and Bert Hamilton were sitting at a table. I was at the bar and on my second beer I heard them getting louder and louder, something about money. Just as Mable the bar maid was getting ready to go over, Hamilton backhanded your Mom across the face. Blood flew and Mable grabbed a bar towel. Hamilton was all sorry and helped your Mom outside...I thought you knew."

Lenny's face burned. He thanked Slats, jumped in the pickup, and turned onto Stimson. At his Mom's house, he bounded up the steps and burst into the living room. His mother was sitting in a rocker, watching a small TV. The Bible rested in her lap. Her lower lip was swollen, and it looked like there was a small berry in the middle of it.

"Lenny, what's wrong?"

"What's happened to your lip?"

"Oh, that. I fell out of bed, split my lip, and had to have a stitch put in. It's all right."

He looked doubtful.

"Lenny, it's all right. I'll be back at work on Friday: I didn't want to go in not looking my best."

He was stymied: he didn't believe her, but he didn't want to contradict her, either. And he had to get back to the farm. As he said goodbye at the door, she opened her Bible. "Remember, son, the Psalmist wrote in 141:3 'Set a guard, O Lord, over my mouth; keep watch over the door of my lips!' God will provide."

Lenny called Denny, but they didn't know what to do.

A month later that changed.

One night Slats called Lenny and said he'd seen Hamilton whacking on Virginia again. Lenny roared into town and found his mother in bed. She had a hard time breathing: her ribs ached and her nose kept bleeding. He took her to the hospital. Hamilton was nowhere around. The next day Lenny checked on her. No broken ribs, but they would be sore for awhile; the doctor had to put two stitches inside her nose. Lenny took her home.

He helped her get settled, ordered a meal to be delivered from the Burger Baron...and Fries, and brought her the Bible. Before he left, she read Second Corinthians 12:9 "But he said to me 'My grace is sufficient for you, for my power is made perfect in weakness. Therefore I will boast all the more gladly of my weaknesses, so that the power of Christ may rest upon me.'" He opened the door. "Son, do you understand? God will provide."

"Yes, Mom."

He called Denny and they formulated a plan.

Hamilton came back from wherever he had gone, all contrite and full of honey. The first thing the twins had to do was to get their mother out of town.

Susie and her mother Carol had taken Virginia out to eat at The Hearth, a steakhouse four miles north of Caseyville. Hamilton came along; Susie and Carol liked Virginia; they found Hamilton distasteful.

Because of their feelings for Virginia, it was easy for Denny to get the two women to take her to Fargo for a long weekend of pre-wedding shopping, including a wedding dress. Virginia was delighted they'd asked her. It made her feel that she was an important part of Denny's life.

On Saturday night, Hamilton clocked out at Menninger Motors and walked to the Burger Baron...and Fries for supper. The twins watched him. Afterward he made a few stops at the Captain's Quarters, the Royal Flush, and Guthrie's; he soaked up a few suds in each bar and then headed for home.

When he turned onto Dakota, Lenny sped by him and a block north let Denny out, then circled back and crawled along behind a slightly weaving Hamilton. As he walked along the farm machinery lot north of Menninger Motors, Denny stepped out, smacked his head with a flat leather sap filled with lead shot. As Hamilton slumped, Denny grabbed him and pushed him into the pickup. The entire operation took seven seconds.

Lenny drove north to just past the old church on the corner of Dakota and Beebe and turned in. He parked behind some shrubs on the east side where no one would see the truck. It was a new moon; darkness was part of the plan.

They hauled Hamilton inside, through the door they had previously jimmied. The church had been constructed by a small congregation years before, but had been abandoned as the members died or moved away. The building had no stained glass or anything valuable once the pews were sold and removed. They tied him up and lashed him to a short pew that had been used by the choir, but was too small for any buyer to want it. They put a gag in his mouth and a hood with eye holes over his head. They waited.

Soon Hamilton moved, then let out a groan. After he was fully awake, they turned on some lanterns. None of the light would be seen outside because they had spent part of the previous night darkening the windows with cardboard. The twins had put on black hoods.

They unbuckled Hamilton's belt and pulled his pants and shorts down around his ankles.

Lenny went outside and came back with a squirming bag, three containers, and some rags. He walked up to an old oak communion table nobody had wanted. "IN REMEMBRANCE OF ME" was carved on one side. Lenny handed the bag to his brother and poured the contents of the container on the table. It was a bleach mixture to disinfect the table.

He walked over to Hamilton and held a sharp blade in front of his eyes. Lowering his voice to a whisper, he said, "This is what we do to men who beat up women." Hamilton shifted uncomfortably.

Lenny pulled off the small rope that kept the bag closed. He pulled out a piglet and removed the cord that had kept its mouth shut. Squeals immediately filled the cobwebbed church. He handed the animal to Denny.

Denny turned the animal on its back and held on. Lenny wiped the scrotum with soapy water and dried it with a rag. He poured some dark brown liquid on the scrotum. Much of it ran off onto the rag. He felt around the scrotum, found what he wanted, and squeezed.

The squeals were louder. He took the blade and made a cut not quite an inch long. A little blood fell on the rag placed on the table. He pulled and a little ball with two cords popped out. He cut through the white cord. The piglet was squealing so intensely it sounded like an abused child.

He twisted the ball several times and severed the corkscrewed blood vessel. Then he searched the scrotum, squeezed, and repeated the same procedure. Surprisingly, there was little blood. The squealing was so pitiful and penetrating that Denny almost lost his hold. Observing everything, hearing the almost human wails, Hamilton broke down in tears and hysteria.

Lenny daubed the wounds with the dark brown liquid. He bound the mouth of the piglet and put it back in the bag. He put what he had removed into the bag. He walked out to the pickup.

When he came back, Denny had spread Hamilton's legs and tied them to the pew so that they stayed apart. Hamilton was thrashing around, trying to break loose. Lenny took the blade and squatted between the veiny legs. Denny went behind the pew.

As Lenny moved closer, Hamilton was trying to arch his back, turn his body, and protect what Lenny was coming for. What noise he could make sounded like a beast trapped deep in a cave.

Denny hit him with the sap.

The twins loosened the ropes a little and left the church with their gear. Even with the knots partly undone, it took Hamilton almost an hour to work himself free. He wormed his way through the door, oriented himself, then loped around the building to the street and up the hill.

Denny and Lenny sat in the pickup at the top of the hill. When they saw Hamilton under a streetlight working his way up, Lenny drove to the back of the Menninger Arms, and they walked to some lilacs across Stimson from their mother's house.

Hamilton came down the block and went inside. Lights came on; the twins waited. No vehicles passed; Menninger was asleep. Hamilton hurried to his car with two large suitcases, went back in. Even though it was late for them, the lilacs perfumed the night air.

Hamilton came out with a large box, went in, returned with two smaller boxes, went back inside.

He came out with the TV set. Denny moved, but his brother grabbed his arm.

"That's Mom's TV."

"I know; let it go."

Hamilton backed the car out of the driveway onto the pavement and floored the accelerator. The car leaped forward down Stimson. When it hit the railroad crossing, it almost went airborne. The twins watched the taillights disappear down the hill.

Lenny drove his brother home. They didn't speak very much. Back at Harrington's place, Lenny put the piglet back with its mother.

When Virginia got back and saw that Hamilton was gone, she hardly mentioned it to anyone. She was thrilled to be helping with the upcoming wedding. She was very happy to be asked to help cut the wedding cake.

After Susie and Denny returned from their honeymoon in the Black Hills and Yellowstone Park and got settled, the twins borrowed a farm truck from Mr. Harrington and moved their mother to Caseyville. Mrs. Charles was a widow and had an extra bedroom in her house. She was so diplomatic in asking Virginia to move into her house, that it appeared Virginia was doing the favor. Susie and her mother knew they'd have to watch any drinking, but without Hamilton and with new friends, Virginia hardly drank at all.

After the boys had gotten everything unloaded, and the bed and other things set in place, Virginia hugged each of them. She picked up her Bible and read Philippians 4:6 "Do not be anxious about anything, but in everything by prayer and supplication with thanksgiving let your requests be made known to God."

She adjusted their high school graduation pictures that she had on her night stand. "As I've always said, boys, God will provide."

C. EDGAR BUCKMAN

C. Edgar Buckman wanted his wife and daughter to have the best of everything. Julia and Judith were very grateful.

Around town C. Edgar Buckman was called "Cash" behind his back because he made all small purchases and even some large ones with cash and because no one outside of his wife and daughter knew that his first name was "Cupid," and they were never going to reveal that embarrassment.

"Cash" Buckman had managed the J.C. Penney's Store on Lamborn Avenue in Menninger, North Dakota, since before World War II. That was another reason to call him "Cash" since the "J.C." stood for "James Cash."

He was about as tall as the movie star Mickey Rooney and when people saw *It's A Wonderful Life*, many of them commented how much Cash resembled Henry Travers, who played Clarence the Angel. When Edgar and Julia saw the picture, he wasn't sure that was a compliment. Moviegoers also saw a resemblance between Julia and actress Bette Davis.

Edgar and Julia Vickers had met in Fargo, where he was taking business courses at the Dakota Business College, and she was a waitress at the Fargo Café on Broadway. After he graduated and got a job at the J.C. Penney's Store in Fargo, they were married in a simple ceremony in her home church at Wheaton, Minnesota.

After a period of learning in the Fargo store, Edgar was transferred to the J.C. Penney's in Menninger. He was named as the manager, but when the bookkeeper moved away, he took on that position, also. It was supposed to be temporary, but when Edgar demonstrated he could hold down both jobs, the change was made permanent.

Edgar and Julia bought a small stucco house on Lamborn Avenue at the base of the Hill, the neighborhood where the crème de la crème of Menninger society resided. They held no illusions about ever climbing their way up the social ladder and were content with each other and their small circle of friends. Then Julia was pregnant, a situation they had not anticipated because a doctor had told her it would never happen.

They realized the house would soon be too small and would get even smaller as their baby grew, so Edgar borrowed from the Bank of Menninger, something he hated to do. Then he began to think of the expense of raising a baby, a child, a teen, and eventually a college student. What could he do on his salary?

Edgar's office was a corner mezzanine with a low wall on two sides over which he could see the entire Penney's store. There were four places for customers to make their purchases, but none of them had a cash register. Instead, the clerk would itemize and total the bill and place it and the payment in a metal container hanging from a thin cable which went around a pulley attached to the clerk's counter and a second pulley up on the mezzanine. A button was pushed and the canister went zipping up to Edgar, who would empty it, put in any change necessary, and push a button, sending the canister back.

One day a dollar bill fell out of the canister and onto the floor of his office. As he picked it up, an idea flashed: he made the change and sent it down, took out another dollar from the payment, wrote "Sale discount" on the slip, and subtracted two dollars from the amount. He put the two bills in his pocket.

He knew it would take him a long time to collect enough money to pay off the loan, but it was a start. A little bit every day marked off by "Sale discount" or "Manager's discount" or "Promotional discount" would add up.

Something else added up, too. He was made the treasurer of the Methodist Church Board. That position was a gold mine: he handled all the money and paid all the bills. It was so easy to skim off some of the Sunday collections—who would know?—and keep some of the money from bake sales, church breakfasts and suppers, and the ladies' bazaar.

He decided to form a bookkeeping firm and devote it to church business. When the other churches heard the Methodists brag about how efficient he was and when the price he quoted for his work was so reasonable, they did away with their treasurers and turned their money over to Edgar. Soon he had the money of the Congregational, the Norwegian Lutheran, and the German Lutheran churches at his disposal.

He took the two Pentecostal churches and the Baptist church in, also, but their memberships hardly made it worth his time. The one church he lusted after was the Roman Catholic, but they weren't about to let a Protestant handle their money.

He was also elected the treasurer of the Kiwanis Club. While the service club didn't offer the financial largess of the churches, membership fees and income from projects offered some unofficial remuneration, especially since many people who had lived through the Great Depression still did not trust banks, even with the FDIC. Cash was their answer.

Edgar was able to persuade the Kiwanis to turn their accounts over to his firm. Their lead was followed by the Masons, the Lions, and the ladies' organizations, the Eastern Star and the Royal Neighbors. Every little bit helped.

Things were going along nicely when Julia's mother died. Her father had been dead several years. When she sold the house and car she had inherited as the only child, Edgar had all the money necessary to pay off the bank loan and to take care of the house they had purchased for at least five years.

It was halfway up the Hill and after they refurbished the interior, bought a new Buick to take the place of their old Chevy, and Julia replaced a lot of the clothes she had purchased at Penney's with tonier apparel from the clothing departments of DeLendrecie's and Herbst in Fargo, the Buckmans' status rose, not that Edgar cared, but since it made Julia happy, so was he.

They were not in the inner circle of eminence and prestige, but they were high enough to be invited occasionally to the Hilltoppers' Bridge Club organized by the new doctor John Bedard and his wife Violet, which had four tables of regular members and two "floating" tables of invited guests.

It was a source of pride for Edgar and Julia that their daughter Judith was fully accepted by the Bedard children, Jamie and Melanie. Although they had some misgivings about Jamie's behavior, they, like the other upright residents of Menninger, never dared to say a word against him.

Many of the Hilltoppers even accepted the Buckmans' invitation to dine at the Chuck Wagon, the upscale eating establishment at Sacred Water.

The extra money was coming in steadily when Edgar's mother passed away on the family farm. He and his brother shared her estate equally. It was then he realized he had too much money.

Judith was at Vassar, thanks to his extra income. That alone had raised the Buckmans' status almost to full acceptance. He and Julia no longer had to spend to keep up appearances in their residence or clothing. He stored his cash in some old suitcases in the former cistern in the basement of the house. There was no light there, so he had to use a flashlight. He was the only visitor to the dim room.

When he totaled the amount made up of used bills, he was astounded. And afraid. What about fire? burglers? the IRS? Years before, he had purchased a .38 Smith & Wesson Special—it would stop a thief, but not flames or the feds.

He made up an excuse to go to Fargo. He scheduled it for the day the Eastern Star met; Julia was the president, so he knew she couldn't go. He met with a realtor and closed a deal on a small house on the near north side. Looking out a window the "PIONEER MUTUAL" sign was prominent.

The next weekend he took Julia to Fargo. He let her shop on Broadway, while he rushed to the little house and moved several suitcases into the basement. He knew it was chancy, but better than getting caught with it in Menninger.

When nothing happened, he relaxed and looked forward to the next trip to Fargo with Julia and the new bills he had accumulated.

He called a hardware store on Broadway and ordered a fire-proof safe. When he was informed it was in, he took his wife to Fargo. While she shopped, he picked up the safe, borrowed a dollie, and sped to the little house. He moved the safe down the basement and transferred his ill-gotten gains to it. The ride home was one of satisfaction and relaxation.

Then disaster. The corporate office informed him that the Penney's in Menninger was to be closed. The very next day an accountant turned up and asked to see the books, not the old man that Edgar had been hoodwinking for years, but a sharp-dressed young man with squinty eyes set deep behind his black horn-rimmed glasses.

After a couple days the man peered at Edgar over his glasses and said he would want to speak with him the next day about some things he didn't understand in the books.

The next morning Edgar called the store and told the man he didn't feel well, but would be in that afternoon. Julia was concerned because her husband never got sick, but she busied herself with making an angel food cake for his birthday. She knew he didn't care for angel food, so she made a smaller chocolate cake with cherry frosting for him.

She went out to have lunch with the other officers of the Eastern Star; for dessert they would come to the house and share in the angel cake. He assured her he wasn't hungry, but if he wanted some food, he certainly could make himself a sandwich. With that assurance, she left.

Quickly, Edgar went to the basement and collected what cash he had there. He retrieved the .38 from their bedroom. He pulled two manila envelopes and some regular envelopes from a desk drawer.

He pushed the two cakes to the far side of the dining room table, put one shell in the proper chamber of the pistol, and placed it on his right-hand side.

He began counting out the money and when he reached a certain amount, put it in a pile in the center of the table. He continued to count and pile. After he had the piles arranged and had placed the extra bills in one of the piles, he took out his pen and labeled each envelope: "Casket," "Flowers," "Funeral Home," "Minister," "Organist," "Soloist," "Meal," "Cemetery Association," "Get Judith Home," "Living Expenses," and "Miscellaneous." He filled each envelope with its own pile of bills and put them all in the manila envelope which he placed on the chair beside him.

He marked "Safety Deposit Box" on a smaller envelope and dropped a key in it. He wrote a street address and "Fargo" on another envelope and put a house key inside. He wrote out the combination to the safe and pushed it inside. He put in a note for his wife: "Do not tell anyone." He put the two envelopes into a manila envelope and wrote "Julia, Personal" on it. He took the envelope into the bedroom, placed it in Julia's Bible on her nightstand and walked back to the dining room.

Edgar sat back in his chair and thought. Had he forgotten anything? Finally, he got up and went into the bathroom. A few minutes later he came back out.

When Julia came home, she called out, "Edgar! We're here! Are you decent?" The Eastern Star ladies all trooped in behind her, through the kitchen and into the dining room. They pushed into each other when Julia screamed and fell to the floor onto a pile of white plaster that had come down from the ceiling.

Edgar's head and chest were slumped onto the table, where a pool of blood from his mouth and some from the top of his head had coagulated. Brain, blood, and bone were scattered across the table, leaving traces of red, pink, gray, white, and clear liquid.

The detritus had even infested his cake upon which he had traced in the frosting with a finger "Sorry."

The fluffy white frosting on the angel food cake was strangely pristine.

IT'S A GRAND OLD FLAG

How Terry Maloney became a radical no one in Menninger, North Dakota, could explain, not even his embarrassed parents.

His father was a bookkeeper at Toney Ford; his mother was the secretary/receptionist at the *Menninger Messenger*. Like most of the townspeople, they generally voted Republican, but like most of the town, they abandoned Barry Goldwater in 1964 and cast their ballots for LBJ because they feared the Arizona Republican would expand the war in Vietnam and maybe even cause a nuclear war.

If there was any indication of radicalism in Terry's background, perhaps it was his enthusiastic support for the Kansas City Athletics, a bottom half team. Even when they moved to Oakland in 1967, he was still a fan of the underdogs, but baseball began to fade for him the next year.

In early 1968 France was rife with political turmoil as elements of the Far Left attempted to oust President Charles De Gaulle by joining together in the coming election. The radicals were firmly entrenched in the Paris University at Nanterre. The conflicts engendered by the radical students and intellectuals led to the closing of the University on May 2. A few days later the Sorbonne University was closed. In turn that caused students and teachers in other universities and even high school students to join the radicals.

On May 6 a march in support of the radicals was met by police with tear gas and batons; the radicals responded with paving stones and barricades. Hundreds were arrested.

Tension built. On May 10 another large crowd formed, leading to a conflict with the authorities, barricades, Molotov Cocktails, burning cars, injuries, and arrests. Television broadcast the confrontation around the world. Terry could not get enough coverage, to the consternation of his parents.

Over a million people marched on May 13, including union members, musicians, writers, and politicians. The government reopened the Sorbonne, but the radicals took it over, declaring it a "people's university."

Many workers took up the cause and occupied factories or went on strike.

On May 27 a meeting with nearly 50,000 people demanded the ouster of the present government and new elections. The Left was confident of victory.

On May 29 President De Gaulle fled Paris and went to Baden-Baden, West Germany, to consult with French military officers. The French government became impotent.

The next day around 500,000 marchers went through Paris chanting their farewells to De Gaulle. However, that day De Gaulle returned, assured of the support of the French military. He dissolved the National Assembly and called for an election on June 23. Immediately after the announcement, close to 800,000 supporters of De Gaulle took to the streets.

Revolutionary fervor wilted: workers returned to their factories, students to their books, professors to their lectures. Demonstrations died out. On June 16 the Sorbonne was reopened. In the election De Gaulle and his party experienced the largest parliamentary victory in French history, winning 353 of 486 seats. The revolution was over.

But not for Terry. Learning that the existentialist philosopher Jean-Paul Sartre had supported the students, he ordered a copy of Sartre's *Being and Nothingness*. It came in its black and yellow dust jacket from the Philosophical Library. Terry had read that Sartre believed existence preceded essence; in fact, each human makes his or her own essence, there is no "human" essence because there is no God. In the Introduction he saw a Sartre devoted to existence and abrogating essence. He also saw the despair with which atheism had imbued Sartre. It was the same feeling Terry had developed ever since he had come to believe that evolution as taught in his science classes negated any necessity for a belief in God.

Sartre was looking for something, but it was nothing found in any other Beings, human or otherwise. In fact, as Terry read deeper into the book, he saw that Sartre considered any relationship with other humans, including sexual, was "slime," the ultimate end of the revulsion and loneliness found in existential belief.

In studying existential philosophy Terry discovered that Sartre did make a commitment, despite the logic of his philosophical position that any such commitment was immoral. The commitment was to revolutionary Marxism, the great opponent of the middle class, the bourgeoisie, the "slimiest" of human institutions.

After slogging his way through the vague verbiage of Sartre, who, like many philosophers, hid his meaning behind terms few could understand, or perhaps hid them so they couldn't be understood, Terry turned to Marx.

The Communist Manifesto was as far as he got (*Das Kapital* was too forbidding), but it was enough. Marx's prose was white-hot revolution, compared to the dark, sometimes impenetrable words of Sartre. He saw truth in "Religion...is the opium of the people." He realized why the dominant class, the ruling class in American society—the middle class—must be overcome when he read, "The ruling ideas of each age have ever been the ideas of its ruling class." And he was inspired by "The proletarians have nothing to lose but their chains. They have a world to win. Workers of the world, unite!"

He didn't dare to expose his existential Marxism to the community in which his parents were such staunch bourgeois members, aside from some comments in his history and civics classes and a veiled reference he would make in one of his editorials in *The Muskie*, the school newspaper. It wasn't until he stepped onto the campus of the University in Grand Forks, that his radicalism blossomed.

The Northern Inter-Scholastic Press Association held its annual meeting on the UND campus. As many staff members as possible from the various high school newspapers and yearbooks attended in order to see old friends, renew old rivalries for the various awards (the competition was especially fierce among the staffs from the large Class A schools), and pick up some pointers for improving their publications the next year. An added bonus for the students from the more isolated small towns was a chance to eat at the McDonald's on South Washington.

The violent deaths of some young Americans, shot by Ohio National Guardsmen on the campus of Kent State University, and the incursions into Cambodia ordered by President Nixon to help end the war in Vietnam had campuses across the nation on edge. UND was no exception.

During a break in the NIPA meeting, Terry heard there was a protest on campus. He left the Union building and saw a crowd of angry students. Suddenly, the shouting mass broke into a run and Terry joined them. They were halted by Security in front of a building which Terry heard was ROTC. Student leaders were demanding the ROTC commander appear. Terry joined them in their chants.

A hand grasped his shoulder. His school advisor told him he had to get back to the meeting immediately or she would recommend he be suspended. He followed her back.

On the bus ride home, he was not caught up in the enthusiasm of his fellow student journalists for their prize-winning efforts—all he could think about was the exhilaration of running with a group of determined radicals.

Before he left for college that fall, Terry ordered two flags of the National Liberation Front, the Viet Cong—top half red, bottom half blue, five-pointed yellow star in the middle. Ever since Pearl Harbor, the Nakamura family had two American flags in holders on either side of the entry to their Menninger Café. They were loyal Japanese-Americans.

Early one morning Terry replaced the Stars and Stripes with that of the NLF. When the early morning coffee drinkers appeared at the entry to the café, they were shocked. The fire siren was sounded, the cops and firefighters were called out, and the mayor declared martial law, illegally. People thought there had been an actual invasion. Eventually, it was seen as a ruse and things settled down, but not before it was noised about that the perpetrator would be lucky if he just got by with tar and feathers.

That fall Terry moved to UND. At a freshman dance in the Union Ballroom, he met a girl named Candy from Center City. Although it was only sixty miles from Menninger, they didn't know each other. As they danced, he felt an attraction to her. She wasn't a raving beauty, but she wasn't ugly, either, and unlike the girls in Menninger, she seemed interested in him.

A few days after they had gone to a movie and then stopped by the Golden Arches, where he bought her a Big Mac and fries, he decided she would be the one he'd have his freshman sexual experience with. He had never had sex, but he didn't think it would be that difficult, just get started and let nature take its course.

Later that Saturday night, they walked hand-in-hand to the large grassy area south of the girls' dorms, fondly nicknamed "Bare Butt Park." There were little copses of trees and plantings of shrubs and flowers that gave plenty of privacy, and the sound of the coulee and its nightlife was romantic in a way. The one problem was that newcomers had to avoid those spots already occupied, not always easy in the dark.

Terry put a blanket on a slightly sloping piece of ground and he and Candy lay down. Both of them knew why they were there, but each was hesitant to start. Once they did, nature did take its course. Terry's first carnal experience was so exciting. Candy seemed more experienced, but he thought that was good. Afterwards, they lay in each other's arms; he gave out with the obligatory "I love you," to which she murmured something indistinct.

Sunday night was warmer. They met and went to the same spot. Terry wasn't feeling the same way, and Candy's ardor had definitely cooled, also. Almost immediately after the coupling, they walked silently out of the park. Their "good nights" were quickly finished and they parted.

As he showered, Terry replayed what had happened. The heat of the night, the sweat from their bodies, the female smells, his own smells, their genital juices, his semen—it was all so slimy. Sartre was right: sexual intercourse requires a body, a body limits our freedom, and we drown in slime. Terry shuddered and turned the shower hotter.

Monday night was perfunctory. They met, they came, they left. Terry once again was repulsed by the slime.

They did not see each other for a week, then just once in passing. He nodded to her, but didn't get a response. She had moved on; so did he.

He turned from the existentialist to the revolutionary.

He attended talks by the leftwing Catholic priest who had been protesting the Minuteman missile sites in eastern North Dakota and counseling young men on avoiding the draft.

He tried to speak with the short, pudgy young woman with black horn-rimmed glasses who stood in front of the Memorial Union for a half hour every noon, dressed in black. On rainy days she had an umbrella. However, she never spoke to anyone, just held up her sign, "STOP THE WAR."

He organized a group of radicals and they had coffee three times a week in the Union. To discuss ways to overthrow the pigs, the Man, the capitalists, the System, the whatever the speaker saw as oppressive.

It was a mixed group: a Maoist from Chicago, a Socialist, two Catholic pacifists, two members of the Women's Liberation Front, two anarchists who wanted the legalization of marijuana, four members of SDS, a Vietnam vet who seemed to have had more time for drugs than fighting, a wannabe Black Panther, two draft dodgers, and a kid who just wanted to hook up with one of the women's libbers, the not-Lesbian one.

The discussions started on a hot note, when the women's libbers demanded non-sexist language from everyone. Once that was resolved,

Terry tried to focus on ways to bring about a revolution, without any particular system in mind to replace the present structure. Those discussions dragged on into a second week, then week three, then nine of the members said they wouldn't be coming anymore.

Terry was panicked. Fumbling for a way to keep his revolution going, he stammered out a plan for a motorcade protest in eastern North Dakota. It just came into his mind, but it was enough. All the members were enthusiastic again, including the Libbers as long as one of the drivers was female.

They decided the first protest would be against the war in Vietnam. They ordered flags and made preparations, including packing lunches, which the two women refused to do.

On a Saturday in mid-October the eighteen started out in three vehicles. They turned off the Interstate onto the East Highway and pulled into a parking lot behind a church in Norton. They unfurled their flags, the kid got out a second-hand bass drum, and they walked across the East Highway onto Indian Avenue, which was basically a gravel street.

They marched in time to the drum beat between grain elevators to the left and residences and then the business district on the right. "Ho-Ho-Ho Chi Minh, the NLF is gonna win!" they shouted. The bright NLF flags fluttered in the sunlight. The two Catholics carried an American flag, but kept it dipped. "One-two-three-four; we don't want your dirty war!"

The bars were closed and many of the old buildings were empty. The marchers came to what must have been a bank at one time and turned around. They started south. Some elevator men came out, took a look, and went back inside. The same at a garage. No residents appeared on a porch or at a window. All-in-all, their march was a failure. They piled into the cars.

Their next stop was Haugen. On the way the Maoist kept bemoaning the fact that the peasants just didn't understand. They bumped over some railroad tracks, turned onto Roberta Avenue, and drove a bumpy piece of pavement into town.

They parked in a grocery store parking lot, got their flags and drum, and marched up Roberta. Happy with the name of the street, the two young women began, "Woman Power! Woman Power! Smash patriarchy!" until Terry quieted them. "This is an antiwar march. We'll do your thing later."

There were a lot more people on the streets than in Norton. They gawked at the marchers, who turned around opposite the water tower and came back. They added to their chants, "Two-four-six-eight; we don't want your greed and hate!"

The Maoist was not happy; the peasants were not rising up as he had hoped, and he saw plenty of them on the sidewalk, snickering and whispering about the marchers. He left the group and walked up to an old farmer in bib overalls. "Don't you see that this is your chance to throw off the running dog bankers and capitalists who keep you in chains. Join us."

The old man hit him in the eye.

He reeled back into the group, holding his face and moaning. The marchers hurried to their cars, fearing a pursuit, but all that followed them were jeers and hoots.

The women refused to help the Maoist, so the pacifists looked him over and said it was nothing. He denied it and sulked against a back door.

McDougall was the next stop. They pulled off at a gas station and started their march. They went north two blocks, but turned around when they saw a cop car parked in the next block. Their chants grew quieter, and when two farmers came out of a bank, the march disintegrated in a mass of bodies running for the vehicles, with the drummer pleading, "Don't leave me!"

They ate lunch on a bluff overlooking the Divide River, then drove over the glacial hills onto the Flats and into Menninger. They stopped at a gas station on the Gold Star Highway, gassed up, and used the facilities. They drove down Villard Avenue and stopped in front of the courthouse.

They had passed a group of boys on the school playground. When the boys saw them get out of their cars, they sauntered over. "Are you guys hippies?" "What's that smell?" (The anarchists had ridden together and smoked their own protest.) "Are you girls really girls?"

At that last remark the women's libbers yelled, "Get outa here!" "Get lost, ya little male creeps!" A couple SDSers faked a run at the boys, who scattered amid a volley of cursing.

A cop came out of the courthouse and stood on the top step. Terry knew him and turned away. The march began; the chanting and the bass drum were loud. They crossed the tracks; people on the streets were watching. The Blackstone Theatre marquee read *Patton*.

They passed Chicago Street and stopped at the corner of Villard and Dakota. Some people from the Amazon Lanes Café came out to see them. People emerged from the American Legion, too, but when they heard the chants, they went back inside.

This was Terry's big moment; he had to do something revolutionary or be lost in slime forever. He stood in the intersection, held up his arms, and quieted the marchers. Speaking briefly, he denounced the war and asked for support from the good people of Menninger.

He called over an anarchist and a pacifist, got a lighter, and lit the American flag on fire.

It happened that the American Legion was holding its annual checkers tournament so the place was packed with Legionnaires, area residents, and wives, as well as some Auxiliary women. Word came in and the vets poured out. They slammed into the marchers like American tanks hit the Germans in the Battle of the Bulge. World War I and II, Korean, and Vietnam vets saw the flag their buddies had died for charred on the pavement. If enemy shot and shell at Belleau Wood, Omaha Beach, Pork Chop Hill, Khe Sahn, couldn't stop these men; if enemy bombs and torpedoes had failed; if life as a POW hadn't killed them, the motley marchers had no chance. Punches, kicks, strangleholds, even Jim Klindworth, an old Navy veteran standing in his walker whacking away with somebody's cane. Some wives and Auxiliary members obliged the women's libbers with a little female fury. A Vietnam vet crashed the drum over the kid's head, pulled it down around his arms, and socked him in the nose. Klindworth's cane raised a huge knot on Terry's forehead.

The cop who had followed the march at a distance and had stood on the Villard-Chicago corner observed the flag burning and subsequent melee, got into his car, and headed back to the courthouse. The vets and their wives disappeared into the American Legion. The marchers dragged themselves up Villard. Their bloody retreat left behind the battered drum and the NLF flags. Later that night the flags were gathered, taken to the back of the Legion, and urinated on. The next day they were thrown into the garbage dump east of town and left to rot. What remained of "Old Glory" was given a Legion retirement and disposal ceremony.

The marchers were left to their own devices. Bones and noses would have to be set; wounds bound up; but first they had to get to Grand Forks. On the way to the courthouse, Terry lost them all. None of them wanted anything more to do with him.

When they reached the cars, there were tickets on each windshield: two for expired license tabs and one for being in a "No Parking" zone.

The gang of boys was gone, but the cars had been egged, with yolks and whites sliming down the sides.

THE ISLAND

After Rory O'Connell left Vietnam, he didn't dwell on the experience he had endured there. All he could think about was Holly Lawrence.

He was disappointed that his mission in 'Nam hadn't turned out better. He had volunteered for a program designed to eliminate the leadership of the Viet Cong operating in the South. Support for the program dwindled after the Tet Offensive and media-driven public opinion turned against American involvement in Southeast Asia.

"The past is prologue," as they say; he had a new life to look forward to in the States. After a brief visit with his family, relatives, and friends in his hometown of Menninger, North Dakota, he headed for the West Coast. He stayed with his cousin Marjorie Ablington and her husband Peter Bruce in Panorama City before he got his own place in Glendale.

He drove a delivery truck, started in a Jack in the Box at the counter and worked his way up to manager, learned meat-cutting and went to work at a Vons. There he watched and learned, took a management course, and ended up as a manager. Years of work, but little satisfaction.

Women came and went. Nothing serious. He ended it or she ended it; the result, he was alone. Even with a girl like Cheryl from Toluca Lake—honey-colored hair, trim figure, classic cheekbones, slender nose, humorous. And she was intelligent, an M.D., family practice doctor. They went together for three years. But Rory was like John T. Unger, the guy in the F. Scott Fitzgerald short story "The Diamond As Big As the Ritz," who was very critical when it came to women. Any defect, such as a thick ankle, a hoarse voice, a glass eye, and the woman became history.

Cheryl had no such physical defects, but there was something wrong—she wasn't Holly. He realized that one night as he lay in that twilight-tinged emptiness that arrived just after his orgasm and before sleep. After making love, Cheryl always wanted to cuddle, so he had his arm around her, listening to her light breathing. It was then he realized he was thinking of Holly. Cheryl's warmth turned cold against his skin.

The next day was Sunday and he begged off doing anything. He knew he was doing Cheryl no favor by staying with her physically and deserting her emotionally.

"Cheryl, I have to leave."

"Where to, the store?"

"No, I have to get out of L.A. I have to get away, away from you, away from everything. I'm no good for you."

By that time she was crying. He grabbed a few things and went to a Holiday Inn. When she was at work the next day, he quit his job, packed up some traveling gear, left a note for Cheryl to do anything she wanted to with what he left behind, and went to the Crocker National Bank for some money. He left his account open and was surprised at how much his savings had accumulated.

He hitchhiked to the Los Angeles rail yards and hooked onto a long freight which he rode to the Tehachapi Loop, where the train slowed and he dropped off.

He spent the summer in the Tehachapi Mountains, exploring among the incense cedars, white firs, black oaks, canyon live oaks, valley and blue oaks, Coulter and gray pines; scaring up cougar, coyotes, fox, racoons and being treed by a herd of feral pigs; and watching the effortless soaring of a California condor. When he needed them, he went into Tehachapi for supplies and headed back into the uplands.

Sometimes he heard game wardens and fire watchers on his tail, either fearful of poachers or fire starters, but he easily evaded them with his jungle-training. Besides, this was California, so everyone just enjoyed it and didn't complicate matters by bringing in the dogs, which could have routed him out.

Eventually, he became another piece of fauna. During the winters, he watched the skiers and the artsy people in Tehachapi, and then he was out to the mountains again. He did venture onto the Mojave once, but got so dehydrated, he almost didn't make it back. The remaining years he was in California were as a mountain man.

The novelist Thomas Wolfe said, "You Can't Go Home Again," but one night Rory decided to. The next morning he came down from the mountains, took a few things from his room, and went to the Loop.

With just about every train piggy-backing its load, it was hard to find an open car, but eventually he did. He threw in his bindle and launched himself from the ballast into the boxcar. Just as he was settling in, a man came in the open door. He was young and glared at Rory with drug-addled eyes. He stood swaying with the car, fumbling in his pocket.

His hand came out. With a knife. "O.K., old man, gimme all your dough!" He started forward.

Rory got up. He walked forward. The knife pointed at his gut. He flashed out his left arm. The knife hand was swept away. Rory hit the kid in the nose with the heel of his right hand. The kid went down. Blood everywhere. Rory dragged him to the edge of the car. He pushed the kid out.

When he looked back, he saw the kid trying to stand. His clothes were dark; his face was scarlet. Rory went to his corner and fell asleep.

It took him several trains before he got to Menninger. In fact, the trains rarely stopped there anymore, so he went to Sacred Water and hitchhiked on the Heinz and Gold Star highways.

He walked down Villard to his old home. It wasn't there; someone had built a duplex on the lot. None of his family was still in Menninger, but he hadn't expected the house to be gone.

He hurried down the street, no lingering; his little sister Theresa had been molested on that block.

The old gymnasium was gone, replaced by an empty lot. What a great Class Night the Class of 1962 had put on.

That wasn't all. The town was changed so much. Some of the buildings were gone—Helgo's Liquor Store, the Arvilla Creamery, the Oleson House, the Menninger Arms Hotel and Café, the Cock-a-Doodle Drive-In, the Good 'n' Hot Drive-In, Blackie's Service Station, the Golden Crust Bakery, where he'd worked.

Other buildings were still there, but empty, some of them boarded up—the church his cousin Chris Cockburn had attended on the west side of town; the old bank burdened with what he heard was a leaking roof that had ruined the interior; the Melva Cunningham Contracting Company building, Melva dead herself.

But the Amazon Lanes, the Blackstone Theatre, the Chevy dealer, all pressed on, along with a new bank and the one grocery store, when there used to be four. The Waterman Auditorium was standing on the same corner, and he wondered if they still had roller skating on Saturday nights.

He got an apartment and looked up his cousin Chris Cockburn. When they went to the Menninger Café for coffee, Chris brought Dotty Zeltinger Wright, a girl he had been sweet on for awhile in high school. Rory was happy for Chris, but felt miserable thinking about Holly.

He went to the new bank, very modern, and had his money transferred from the Crocker, which had been taken over by Wells Fargo. He bought a small white frame house that for some reason lost in time stood at a forty-five degree angle to Gregory Avenue. It was near Orland Finkle Park, where he spent a lot of time watching people having fun and talking with some of them about...well, nothing important.

He got a part-time job as a meat cutter at the grocery store and another one at a C-Store on the Gold Star; bought a Chevy from a man he remembered by name, but who didn't recognize him; and dated a few women, all divorcées. None of them serious on his part; the last woman asked him in bed if she could stay the night. When he said no, she got dressed, walked out without a word, and that was the end of that.

He drove to the Twin Cities to see his folks and came home depressed, they had aged so much, especially his father. Then he died. At the Funeral Mass, Rory was the only member of his family who did not go up for Communion.

He had lost his Catholicism in Vietnam; somewhere between the death agonies and the tortured screams, it had dwindled away. All his sisters and brothers--Mary-Margaret, Liam, Kathleen, Maureen, Kevin, and Theresa—were married and had kids. And were still Catholic.

At the funeral he talked with his cousins Roger, called "Boy," and Tommy Cockburn, not Catholics, but married and fathers and happy.

He came home feeling worse than ever. He told his employers he would only work for them during the winters. They agreed; they needed him. He would spend the nice weather tramping central North Dakota: in the glacial hills; climbing the few buttes such as Buffalo Hump, Red-Tail Ridge, Thunder Butte, and Bunch Grass Hill; around the lakes and sloughs, following the rivers; wondering about glaciers, bison herds, prairie fires, mighty things, but now all gone.

He'd stop in the little towns, aspirations slowly dying. The residents, almost all of them old. The buildings even older.

His mother died. The funeral was even more depressing. Afterward Liam handed him a note. His mother had written it. After the interment in St. Andrew's Cemetery north of town, he opened the note in his car. "Son, don't forget Holy Mother Church." He cried.

But he didn't go back to the Church. He worked, he tramped, he visited with Chris and Dotty, and a few old friends. And always she was there—Holly.

One spring day while he was airing out his sleeping bag and making plans to hike out to Big Sam Lake and Buffalo Hump, he was interrupted by a knock on the door. Holly. Older, of course, but he could never forget her face. Makeup trying to hide wrinkles. Her golden-brown hair with highlights, her body somewhat thicker, but Holly, always Holly.

"Aren't you going to invite me in, stranger?"

He felt awkward, just as he did as a teenager when they were together. "I'm sorry." He gestured her in. They sat on the sofa and talked. Their families (she had two grown daughters and three grandchildren), their lives since high school (she was divorced; "The little rat cheated on me!"); their current lives (she was living on a great divorce settlement and traveling). He let her do most of the talking; he loved her voice. He described the jobs he'd had, life in the mountains, and his wanderings around central North Dakota. He said nothing about Vietnam or about the women he'd been with. He was embarrassed, but she seemed to be listening.

He took her to dinner at the Menninger Café and insisted on paying. She got the tip with a ten-dollar bill.

They went out to St. Andrew's and stood beside the family graves. She even teared up, looking down at the graves of her mother and father.

She wanted to see some old girlfriends, so he spent some of the afternoon cleaning every conceivable spot and surface in the house. He even changed the bed linen.

She wanted to go to the Chuck Wagon, a ritzy restaurant at Sacred Water. He was surprised it was still open. She drove them in her Chrysler 300. She ordered for them, lobster and steak. The steak was the best he'd ever tasted, but he had never tried lobster. She got a good laugh, trying to show him how it was done. She put everything on her credit card. He didn't even have one.

They drove home with a moon waxing toward full, brightening the landscape into semi-day and reinforcing the feelings he had for her ever since they had broken up.

At home without a word, they went into the bedroom. Passion unpent. Exploration of the flesh. Holly's taste, touch, smell. The wasted years unwound. Mutual culmination. Exhaustion. But not the emptiness that had haunted him in the past.

"I need to shower."

"All right. I'll help."

"No, silly man. Wait until I'm done."

He watched her tip-toe to the bathroom. She turned on the light, revealing her body, her flesh, the woman he loved, would never stop loving. She shut the door. He waited in bed, her smell rampant, and thought of his new life, their new life.

She came out and finished drying off. She toweled her hair again, went to her purse, and took out a brush. He waited for her. He liked watching her hands, her hair.

She put on her panties, then her bra. He wondered. She slipped on her thin white top. "What's going on?"

She pulled on her gray-checked skirt. "You know what's wrong with you, Rory?"

He stared at her.

"You haven't changed since high school. You had no ambition then, and you have no ambition now." She put on her light gray sweater. She sat on the bed and put on her shoes. She stood and looked down on him. "Goodbye, Rory."

He heard the front door shut. He put his head on his pillow and tried to die.

He didn't leave his house for five days; he didn't eat for five days; he didn't drink for five days. Late on Saturday evening he walked down Gregory to the park. Walking beside the Jacques River, he remembered a raft he, Liam, Chris, and their friend Ronnie Kerr had built and floated it down the river, being pulled for a time by a big snapping turtle they had hooked. He looked across where two old wagon wheels had stood and where the five Bouvette children and another boy had drowned. He crossed the Gold Star and continued east, past where his brother Liam almost drowned when a storm hit the raft.

Soon he passed Sullivan Point over on the north bank where the three Sullivan sisters had drowned during an Independence Day picnic around the turn of the century.

He came opposite an island, maybe two hundred feet long by fifty feet at its widest, almost entirely surrounded by reeds and overgrown with snakeberry bushes and tall grass. It was in some reeds on the west tip of the island where searchers found the body of little Yvonne

Bouvette. He had been careful to keep low and out of sight as much as possible. He looked around, took off his shoes and clothes, bundled them, and held them on his head with one hand. He entered the water and stroked with one arm for the island. It was spring, but the water was cold.

He walked onto the island and smashed down a place near the east end, away from the highway. There was a small beach there and the bushes were thinner. He lay down on his clothes and prepared to die. It might take a week, but he was prepared. No one ever came to the island; it was too small and empty and marshy. His body might not be discovered for years. He was cold, but maybe that would help the dying process. The moon was waning, but still almost full. It would be nice to die under such a moon…Dying wasn't so hard, just cold…

Something woke him. A scratching sound. He listened. It came from the beach. He crawled forward and parted the reeds. A female snapping turtle was digging in the sand. He watched. It took her awhile. He waited, postponing death.

When she was done, he could tell it had been difficult for her, exhausting. She had more to do. He watched as eggs were deposited in the hole. It took tedious time. She didn't quit. She finished just after sunrise. She used her hind legs to bury the eggs. She slowly made her way to the water and disappeared.

Without warning, he didn't want to die. He bundled his clothes and swam to the south bank. He waited for the chill air to dry his body. He tried to comb his wet hair with his fingers. The sun slowly warmed him. He put on his clothes, his socks, his shoes; they felt good. He walked the river back to the Gold Star. The bell for eight o'clock Mass sounded from St. Andrew's on the hill.

He looked up and saw the cars arriving, the people hurrying in. He began to run; he didn't want to be late. By the time he reached the door, he was out of breath and seeing black; he had to rest near the holy water.

He dipped his fingers and made the Sign of the Cross. He saw an empty pew and walked to it. He genuflected and put down the kneeler.

On his knees, he made the Sign of the Cross. He thought of how he should pray—for his father and mother, his family, and, yes, most especially for himself...

"Our Father, Who art in heaven..."

"HELLO, MY NAME IS LYDIA LEE"

"Hello. My name is Lydia Lee and I'm in Third Grade. I want to welcome you to our Christmas concert."

She was small for her age, but that was not unexpected, since her parents were smaller than average. That didn't stop her father; he played football and gained the name "Bulldog" with his lack of fear against much larger opponents. Her mother Laurie Ann was cute and that translated into being a cheerleader, Homecoming Princess, and class officer all four years at Menninger High School.

Lydia Lee was the darling of the older ladies—shy, petite, blonde, blue-eyed, all peaches-and-cream, she reminded them of their own granddaughters or how they wished their granddaughters looked and acted.

She was the pride of her own grandparents. Bulldog's folks, Oliver and Agnes, lived on a grain and cattle farm; Laurie Ann's parents, Bill and Anna, ran a local drug store. They showered Lydia Lee and her two sisters with affection and presents—the girls always had the newest in clothing and shoes and the most educational in toys, games, and books.

Lynda was four years older than Lydia Lee. Looking a little too much like Bulldog to be pretty, she was athletic and independent. Even though she weighed a little over nine pounds at birth and her parents had been married just seven months, all the grandparents insisted she had been premature.

Lynette was two years older. An outgoing tomboy, in her high school years she excelled on the basketball court, running track, and playing softball. Unlike Lynda, she could sing and went to the State Music Contest three years.

Life was good; the three sisters thrived.

"Hello. My name is Lydia Lee and I'm a four-year student of Mrs. Welter. I would like to welcome you to the annual piano recital of all her students."

Although she was only an eighth grader, Lydia Lee was the best of Mrs. Augusta Welter's seventeen students, even better than the three high school girls who had stuck out the strict regimen demanded by Mrs. Welter.

Still shy, Lydia Lee would speak and perform in public if her teachers or parents demanded it—she wanted to please people, even though her heart pounded and her legs felt as though they had tremors.

Popular with her classmates, she had been elected class secretary. She had two best friends—Marijo, tall and freckled, but burdened with ears a little too large; a budding scientist, but afraid of snakes; her mother had been a Homecoming Queen; and Betsy, who kept her classmates laughing with her great sense of humor, which was never mean; sometimes she had trouble with the "s" sound, but if she caught it, she turned it as humor onto herself; she liked cooking and eating what she made, so she was overweight and always had been. They called themselves the Three, but were friendly to everyone.

Lydia Lee's eighth grade and freshman years were the best years.

"Hello. My name is Lydia Lee and I'm running for Student Council secretary. I hope you will vote for me."

She won; Marijo, who was running for treasurer, lost. It took awhile for Lydia Lee and Betsy to cheer her up.

Actually, it was Lydia Lee who needed the cheering. Bulldog and Laurie Ann were fighting. Lynette and Lydia Lee would lie in their beds and listen to them yelling and cursing at each other. It was terrible. She would accuse him of seeing another woman; he would deny it. Sometimes he would slam out of the house, and Lydia Lee was afraid he would never come home; then she was afraid he would.

At first Lydia Lee had Lynette to talk to; Lynette would hug her and tell her things would work out. After Lynda heard one of the fights on a visit from college, she never returned. In her junior year and with Lynette in college, Lydia Lee was alone with the sounds of parental combat.

Her school work dropped off a little, but neither Bulldog nor Laurie Ann noticed. It wasn't until she confided in Marijo and Betsy, that she turned herself around academically. Partly relieved of her burden, she hit the books and boosted her grades. She thanked God for the good friends she had.

She spent hours in the evening talking on the phone, first with one of the Three and then with the other. Afterward she would pray that God would heal the anger of her parents and then fall asleep. Usually on a tear-wet pillow.

Then it happened. Bulldog's parents had moved off the farm, and he took over its management entirely. It was the spring of her junior year. At breakfast, she heard her Dad tell her mother he had plowing to do, so he wouldn't be home until late. He kissed Lydia Lee and left. Kisses for Laurie Ann were as dead as last year's leaves.

Laurie Ann went to her parents' drug store, where she had been clerking as soon as Lydia Lee was old enough to be home alone after school. She didn't need the money, just the independence.

Her suspicions were aroused, so she told her father she needed an hour or two off, drove over to Villard Avenue, and picked up her mother. They went out to the farm.

The pickup was beside the machine shed, the tractor and plow were in the yard, but Bulldog wasn't around. The two women walked in without knocking. There was no one on the first floor, but they heard noises on the second. They climbed the stairs, making creaky-stair sounds, but the noises never stopped. They listened outside the second door. Female sounds; male grunts. Laurie Ann opened the door: two naked people making a human with two backs. Laurie Ann's mother screamed. The woman screamed. Bulldog cursed.

Laurie Ann slammed the door. Coming into town on Chicago Street, they turned onto Villard and stopped at the lawyer's office.

"Hello. My name is Lydia Lee and I'm running for Homecoming Queen. I hope you will vote in the election, hopefully for me, but any one of us up here would be a fine Queen."

She won. Maybe it was because of her looks or personality or talent or maybe because her schoolmates felt sorry that her parents had gotten divorced. Who knows what feelings lurk in the teenage heart?

But she lost, also. Marijo had been certain she would be the Queen. She would wear the crown and hold the flowers in the picture in the yearbook, just like her mother.

Lydia Lee couldn't understand the sudden chilly indifference Marijo had for her. Phone calls shortened or not returned; no talking by the lockers; no walking to class together. Betsy, who hadn't even been nominated for Queen, knew. Eventually, she told of Marijo's thwarted ambition. Lydia Lee found Marijo to apologize. Marijo called her a snake and said she never ever wanted to speak to her again. Tears and restless sleep were Lydia Lee's bed companions.

Even though things weren't the same, never could be the same, she had Betsy as a close friend, her piano, and her studies. She was going to try hard to make up for the B's she'd received during the other rough time.

She had gone to the prom for three years straight. The first boy, her classmate, walked her to the door, said good night, and fled as though Bulldog stood behind it with a shot gun. She thought it funny.

Her second date actually attempted a good night kiss, but most of it ended up on her chin. It looked like he was going to make a second try, but chickened out and hustled to his car.

Her junior year she went with a boy she didn't really like, but he had asked her first. She let him kiss her several times, then said good night, and went in. He told stories about how far he'd gotten, but no one believed him.

After the prom and a change of clothing her senior year, the athletic boy who was her date took her to Perkins in Kingston, where they had breakfast with several other couples from MHS. On their way back, they stopped in the grove surrounding the athletic field south of Menninger. They made out in the front seat; she didn't care for his tongue. Then he produced a bottle of liquid, poured some out the window, and added something else. He handed it to her. She asked what it was. Sloe gin and club soda. "Try it." It was bitter and she coughed. He chuckled. "It'll grow on ya." He took a big drink. He had been on the football and basketball teams and was running track; she had no idea he drank. His mouth had been on the bottle, but she figured they'd kissed so many times that shouldn't make a difference. She drank...a bigger drink...and coughed.

He drank; she drank; they made out. He drank; she drank; she let him feel her breasts. Eighteen years old and it had finally happened. Marijo, Betsy, and she had talked about it many times; it didn't feel like much at all.

Her head felt weird. Then his hand went between her legs. If she didn't stop him, she knew where it would lead. He tried to push her flat; she yelled for him to stop. He didn't. She slapped him and burst into tears.

He sat up, started the car, and spun out on the cinder track, careened onto Chicago, almost hit the curb getting onto Villard, and jammed on the brakes in front of her house. She sat there. He growled, "Get out." She did. He called her a dirty name and roared off. She was sick in the bathroom; her mother helped her into bed.

By that time almost everyone at MHS had a Twitter account. Over Sunday the prom and its aftermath were the main subject of the tweets. Boys' reputations were enhanced; girls ended up as frigid or easy. She was shocked to see she was easy. The tweets kept up two days and then other things popped up: Taylor Swift's latest boy troubles; Selena Gomez and her latest hair style; what was going on with Justin Bieber?

"Hello. My name is Lydia Lee and I want to welcome you to our graduation. Please join me in the Pledge of Allegiance."

In keeping with the temper of the times, the MHS senior class had six valedictorians and three salutatorians. Lydia Lee had worked her GPA up to where it qualified her as one of the tri-sals, but only one of them and two of the valedictorians would give speeches. The names were drawn from a cap; the other six honor students were given different roles.

After the prom night experience, Betsy and she commiserated with each other: Lydia Lee because of her shot reputation; Betsy because no one had asked her. One night Betsy brought some wine coolers; they sat in Betsy's car in the athletic field grove and drank. The world felt better.

Lydia Lee talked to a boy with a reputation for such things and paid him to get her some liquor. The world became more likeable.

She could take it or leave it; during finals' week she never touched the stuff. Didn't that prove it? But it was graduation she dreaded, and she made sure she had a good supply. After the ceremony, she would have to walk out between her father and mother, as though they were one little happy threesome. It was all so hypocritical.

After the divorce, she would spend one week with her mother, then be trundled off to the farm for a week with her father. She didn't like being treated like a dead weight used to balance the scales of justice. She'd heard of a judge who said in such cases, it was the parents who should move back and forth, while any children stayed in one home. She wished the judge lived in Menninger.

Her dislike turned to hate after her mother's boyfriend Chad moved in. She thought he was dirty, ate like a hog, and drank too much. But her mother was drinking too much, also. Her father and the woman that broke up his marriage split up, and he was on his third girlfriend. She was a thin little thing named Trixie, or maybe that was a nickname, always trying to talk to Lydia Lee, but losing her train of thought; maybe she was on drugs.

When Lydia Lee led the Pledge of Allegiance, she lost her place; she was "buzzed." But that feeling helped her walk between her parents with a smile. Before she appeared at the graduation reception at her mother's place, she went to her room and chugged down some vodka. She smiled the rest of the afternoon; people thought she was happy.

As the summer progressed, she followed the lead of the Twitter crowd: her tweets became more raunchy, more profanity-laden. She and Betsy thought it hilarious to tweet words that their mothers would have punished just a few short years before. Then she got a new iPhone for graduation, and it was even more fun, because she could be off by herself, take a slug of booze, and tweet and retweet the worst words she knew.

The comedian George Carlin said there were seven words that couldn't be said on TV. Well, they could be tweeted: two dealing with bodily excrement and fluid, two terms for parts of the female anatomy, a slang term for a fellator, and two with the "F" word. Betsy and Lydia Lee avoided the last two until Judean and her friends entered the picture, then those words became their favorites.

Laurie Ann drove her daughter to Fargo to enroll at the University. Lydia Lee could have driven herself, but her mother wanted some quality time together. It wasn't. Except for some time talking about little nothings at dinner, there was silence, imposed by Lydia Lee and her headphones.

Several weeks later Lydia Lee was informed her roommate was from the neighboring town of Caseyville. Her name was Judean. Lydia Lee knew her slightly. Soon they were tweeting about who would bring what for their dorm room, classes they would be taking, selfies. Then summer was gone.

Bulldog, without his girlfriend who was in treatment, helped her move in. Judean's whole family helped her. After everyone had gone, Judean produced two wine coolers and they toasted their new lives.

"Hello. My name is Lydia Lee and my Power Point is on 19th century immigration into the United States."

College classes were a lot rougher than those in high school. She could keep up with a lot of study, but Judean and her friends down the hall always wanted her to shop or party with them, so her study time drifted into the early morning hours.

She could handle the reading and since many of the lectures were posted online, she spent a lot of class time texting: she had outgrown Twitter. Still, standing in front of a hundred or so students and speaking was daunting for her; a lot of her natural shyness had returned. She could do it, but only with a little boost from a bottle. Sometimes she was graded down because she would lose her place or slur indistinctly.

Like 99.44 percent of the campus, for that matter of Fargo itself, she and her friends were caught up with football fever. On Friday nights they'd drink to the team. The next day they drank enough to put a "buzz" on and walk to the big Dome, where drinking wasn't allowed. The noise produced by the rabid fans and the band music made Lydia Lee's head pound. Back in the dorm she took a few drinks and lay down to sleep, which came easily since the ringing in her ears blocked out other noises.

What she started to like more and more were the frat parties Judean took her to. Judean and her friends seemed to know everyone. After some parties, they'd get together and tell each other what had happened. Then a new game was introduced: Get the Guy.

At the beginning of a party, each girl was to tell the others which guy she was interested in. After the party they would compare notes and see how far each one had gotten. Soon it became a contest to see how many guys they could have sex with. They made a chart and after each girl's name a big "F" would be written for each conquest.

After three weeks Lydia Lee was the only name without an "F." She felt embarrassed. Back in high school, no "F" would have been a source of pride. For a girl who attended Sunday School and church, went to and then taught Vacation Bible School, and liked going to Bible Camp, it was God's Will to be virginal until marriage. But God had dwindled in her life since the divorce.

The teasing aimed at her wore her down. On Halloween she and the other girls dressed up in funny or scary costumes and headed for a frat. That was where she met Gene. He was a senior, majoring in Agricultural Economics, tall, fair, average looking, but with well-groomed hair and a nice laugh. She pointed him out as her target and walked over. She didn't dare speak, so she just looked at him until he noticed and came over.

"Hi, my name is Gene. Want something to drink?"

Her heart was trip-hammering. "I'm Lydia Lee and I'd like that."

He came back with two Bud Lights. She didn't like beer, but drank it anyway. She started to relax. She asked for something else. He brought a wine cooler. They sat and talked and drank. And drank. He was easy to talk to. Better looking than she had thought.

"It's kinda noisy in here."

"Yeah, hard ta hear."

"We could go to my apartment. It's a couple blocks over. We could walk."

"O.K." She stood up and wobbled. "I guess you'll have to help me."

They both knew why they were there. A few preliminary kisses, and then down to business. She tried to feel something, anything. Then he was done and rolled off. She didn't know what to do. She felt some wetness. "I have to use the bathroom." She was bleeding a little; she hadn't felt any pain.

When she came back, he was very apologetic. "I'm sorry; I didn't know…a virgin."

She told him it was all right. He went into the bathroom and she pulled on her clothes. He said he'd walk her to the dorm; she said to wait. She had to sit on a chair for ten minutes, waiting for her stomach to settle down. Back in the dorm, she was violently ill.

All the girls were thrilled and gave her two big "F's."

She and Gene started going out, which ended up with them in bed, which led to her sleeping over. Sometimes in the morning, she would study Gene as he slept. His hair would be drier and would flip up into a curly wave on top of his head like the Kewpie dolls Grandma Anna kept on her china closet. She realized he was going bald, but didn't know how she felt about it.

She drove home to a thankless Thanksgiving. Both Lynda and Lynette had jobs which they said required them to work; basically, it was an excuse. On Thursday she ate a turkey dinner with her mother and Chad, who watched TV and drank. She helped with the dishes and listened to her mother complain about Bulldog not paying off on the divorce settlement. Betsy and her other friends wanted time with their families; she could hardly wait to get away from hers. Friday was blurry, thanks to the amount of alcohol she drank in her room. Even her mother commented on how much she was drinking, which Lydia Lee thought was pretty hypocritical.

She had to spend Saturday and part of Sunday at the farm with her father and Trixie, eating leftovers and listening to her father complain about Laurie Ann hounding him for money when the farm was almost failing and to Trixie, who kept chirping about how cool it was to be clean.

On the drive to Fargo, she turned on Sirius XM and listened to Bruno Mars, Katy Perry, Pink, Rhianna, Taylor Swift, and Justin Timberlake. She liked songs with good melodies. She wondered if she had tried singing instead of piano, which she had given up, if she could have become a star. She knew she was just as good as some of the performers on *American Idol.*

Gene didn't call. When she went to his apartment, he seemed surprised and said he'd meet her later. When he showed up, he handed her a box, and said they shouldn't see each other anymore. Before she could ask why, he was gone. The box had things she had left in the apartment. The next day she saw him walking with a girl on campus.

Judean and the other girls told her how sorry they were, but she should move on. The "F" chart was gone; over Thanksgiving Judean and Ashley had reignited relationships in their home towns, Emily and Sami were serious about two boys on campus, and Sarah was still looking, but had two prospects.

She got a text from her father; the farm was in such bad shape he wouldn't be able to pay for her Sirius radio anymore or even to send her the hundred dollars he had been giving her every month as spending money. He would still pay half her tuition.

Finals came and went; she thought she had done well, and during the week didn't even drink that much. When the tests were over, it was time to party. The other girls all had dates, so when she heard of a house party off campus, she wandered over.

It was wild; wilder than any frat party. College guys, biker dudes, guys off the streets, tats everywhere, piercings where you wouldn't believe. She found a drink and a place to sit. She tried to be pleasant to the guys who talked with her, but resisted any attempt to get her off the couch. She drank some more. Girls were stripping. Then guys were stripping, carrying what looked like a nest of baby birds in their groins.

A blonde boy sat down; he seemed nice. He offered her a drink. "What is it?"

"What do you want it to be?"

She thought that was funny. She drank. When he said they should go upstairs, she had no will of her own. She went. When she turned at the top of the stairs, she saw three figures following them.

They kissed. His hands went to work on her clothes. She had no resistance. He pushed her on the bed. *What's happening? Everything is so dark.* The bed moved. And kept moving. *It shouldn't take this long. Gene never did.* Different male smells, but the bed kept moving. Different male sounds, but the bed kept moving. *I'm so tired. What is going on? What is...*

When she woke up, the house was dark and quiet. She found a bathroom and showered the grunge off her body, off her legs. She got dressed, found her coat, and crept back to the dorm.

Christmas vacation had started.

"Hello. My name is Lydia Lee and there's something wrong with me."

The nurse took her back to an examining room.

Christmas had been even worse than Thanksgiving. Her grades showed up: all B's. She was shocked; she'd only had a couple B's in high school. With grade inflation rampant, she knew a B was really a C. She felt terrible until a little liquor dulled her disappointment. Booze also drew a mist around what had happened at the house party, not that she could remember much or even wanted to remember.

One week with Laurie Ann and one week with Bulldog were bad enough, but her mother could only afford one present, a winter coat, and her father cried when he said he couldn't afford any presents.

That wasn't the worst of it. Oscar and Agnes were in the nursing home and without a long-term care policy, the huge expense was devouring their savings. Both of them cried when they said she shouldn't count on any more money from them. Bill and Anna had moved to Florida. They sent her a card and a check for twenty-five dollars; enclosed was a note: their condo had experienced severe roof damage in a storm, termites were ruining the structure, and their car, house, and her health insurance payments were killing them. They were sorry, but the money she had been getting monthly had to stop.

On New Year's Eve she and Betsy got some liquor, drove to Caseyville for the dance, went in, looked around, and walked back to the car. They parked in a motel parking lot where the car wouldn't be conspicuous, drank, and told each other about how the world sucked.

When she left Menninger, her mother told Lydia Lee she'd have to pay for her iPhone herself, but that she would still pay for her car insurance, half her tuition, and her birth control pills.

Back on campus, Judean and the others seemed uncomfortable around her. She went to two parties, but at each of them, she saw people staring at her and whispering. The one word she heard clearly at both places was "Topo."

She asked Judean what "Topo" meant. Judean asked her friends in for moral support and told her it was short for "Topography." When she didn't understand, Judean said, "It means you're the lay of the land."

Lydia Lee threw herself on the bed and flooded her pillow. Judean and the girls rubbed her back and cooed kind words, but she was still crying when they left.

Then she noticed a vaginal discharge, foul smelling, and a pain when she urinated. She went to Student Health, where she was diagnosed with chlamydia and given the appropriate treatment. She was so mortified, she couldn't speak. The nurse tried to reassure her that many of the young women on campus were dealing with the same thing. And many more were infected and didn't know it. She was lucky; they'd caught it early. It hardly helped.

She remembered in Mr. Lowell's Health class at MHS when they were studying STD's, and he was late to class. She heard kids laughing and saw a note was being passed around. After everyone else had seen it, Dennis Dugan walked up to her and dropped it on her desk. She unfolded it: "LYDIA HAS CHLAMYDIA." The whole class burst out laughing. Her face was blistering, but the worst was Marijo and Betsy were laughing, too.

For three days she wouldn't talk to them, but then apologies made it better. During that time she thought of third grade on the playground. At recess some of the older boys cornered Betsy and a crowd gathered. Marijo and she looked on, wondering. The boys started to chant: "Help! Murder! Police! Betsy fell in the grease! She laughed so hard, she turned into lard! Help! Murder! Police!"

The other kids thought that was hilarious and laughed and hooted. Marijo and she joined them. Betsy ran into the school, crying; her mother came and got her, and she missed the rest of the day. She wouldn't have anything to do with Marijo and Lydia Lee until time wore away the hurt. It had taken six years from the teasing to the note for her really to understand Betsy's pain. That night she had begged God to forgive her for the hurt she had caused her friend.

God hadn't been part of her life since the divorce, but as she walked out of Student Health, she said, "Please, God, help me. Show me the way." Two girls looked at her and she realized she had spoken out loud.

She didn't start going to church, but she did begin her meals with a silent Grace and said her prayers at night. She stopped going to parties and began looking for a job; she realized she'd never had one before, not even babysitting.

One day she went to a McDonald's and saw a sign for Help Wanted. Applications were on-line. She applied by phone; a week later there was a reply.

"Hello. My name is Lydia Lee and I'm here about a job."

The manager, Nick, was dark-haired with a little silver, even though he looked maybe thirty. He sat behind his desk. His look was steady, not hostile, not friendly, just intense. Her mouth felt dry.

"Now, Lydia Lee…is that what you like to be called, not just Lydia?"

"Yes. Lydia Lee."

"We need help; we always need help, but good help, willing help. In return we try to make it worth your time and effort." He looked at his computer screen. "I see you listed no job experience."

"No, I've never had a job."

"No references."

"I never had a boss."

"A minister would do."

She looked down.

"Actually, a clean slate such as yours may be to the good; you'll have no bad habits and will learn the McDonald's way right from the start…Are you on Facebook?"

"No."

"Twitter?"

"I don't use it anymore."

"Would you mind scooting around here and showing me your account?" She found it and sat down. He looked and scrolled; looked and scrolled. "Well, two things stand out; you have a filthy mouth and you drink too much."

She got up to leave. He motioned her back. "Wait a minute." She sat. "I want to offer you the job. However, at McDonald's there is no cursing; customers don't like it and I don't like it. As to drinking, that's your business unless it interferes with my business. Would you like the job?"

Learning from Nick and working with him—he always seemed to be there—made her feel appreciated. It was tough, what with her studies, but he accommodated her work schedule with her college time. Her very first paycheck with her name on it! She felt she had contributed something and had been appreciated.

College and work. Judean and the other girls were there, but not that important anymore. She texted Betsy and once in awhile her parents; that was enough. Nick introduced her to his wife Norine and their three-year old twins, Patsy and Peggy. So cute, blonde like their mother, and very quiet, unlike a lot of the kids she saw at work. Every couple weeks Norine would pick up Nick and they'd go to a meeting. Nick thought Lydia Lee would find it interesting. She suspected it was some conservative church meeting and she wasn't into that.

And then Gene. He texted her one Friday, saying he missed her, thought they were good together, and wanted to see her. She did not respond. She dug out her secret green apple vodka bottle and went to bed with Mr. Smirnoff.

The next morning she was so sick she had to call Nick and tell him she couldn't work. What could he say? When she did come to work on Sunday, she avoided him as much as possible. When they made eye contact, she knew that somehow he knew.

May fluttered in like a sun-dappled butterfly. She had a whole summer. She had her car; her iPhone; her job; she'd live in her little apartment, crummy, but adequate; and then walking under the canopy of elms on University, finished with her last final, she saw the blonde boy from the house party.

She ran the final two blocks, half-memories igniting nausea. *God help me! God help me!* She hadn't let God into her life far enough, so it was her second secret bottle—Smirnoff Grape—to the rescue. Already packed, Judean came in to say goodbye. She moved out while Lydia Lee obliterated everything with darkness.

She was supposed to go to work. She just couldn't. Another call to Nick. Then coming to work. Avoiding his knowing gaze.

At the end of the shift, he called her into his office. "Norine and I have a meeting this week. I strongly encourage you to attend. You can ride with us." Did she have a choice? She agreed.

When they pulled into the parking lot, she saw it wasn't a church. Inside there were dozens of people, people just like she'd meet on the street or in the Mall. People who talked and laughed like people do. Then the meeting started, and some of them got up and revealed themselves, their problems, to everyone. To Lydia Lee that was something shocking and unheard of. Then it happened.

Both Nick and then Norine did the same thing. Lydia Lee was incredulous. They were so nice; their girls were so darling.

That night she went to her apartment; Nick and Norine had helped her move in. Mr. Smirnoff was in the Fargo sewage lagoon. She knelt beside her bed. She prayed her first heartfelt prayer since high school. First for forgiveness, then for her family and friends, then thankfulness for Nick and Norine, and finally with a plea, "God help me." Before she drifted off, she made up her mind.

"Hello. My name is Lydia Lee and I'm an alcoholic."

THE OLD MAN

He liked to sit with the late-fall sun on his legs. On his head was a hat; inside the brim the little chickadee pecked for a seed, flew away to the caraganas, flew back, and pecked again. The old man was hatching a plot.

He thought of his wife, Sarah, long dead. He saw her as a young woman in a thin cotton dress, standing with a hand shading her eyes against the prairie sun, waiting for him, driving the team up the lane, harness jingling, veneered with field dirt, a tractor on hold until after the war. Or she'd be kneeling in the dust, crying over the barn cat he had accidentally runover. Sometimes he saw her introducing the program that marked the end of term for the country school; she looked so proud of her students. Or he would be watching her from the corner of his eye, in church, listening to her sing, rather than sing himself.

He rarely remembered the shrunken, cancer-ridden figure, dying in a hospital bed. The last week at home. Nothing more could be done; she wanted to be home. Every day he took her outside to sit in the sun; Sarah loved the sunshine.

Sometimes he would wonder what she'd look like in Heaven, if he ever made it there.

He hoisted up, grabbed the cane, and made his way into the house. He wondered if the pain in his groin was the mesh working loose again. Out loud he said, "It doesn't matter."

Sold off the farm when she got sick. The money paid for five years of fighting off the Killer, but in the end Death was the winner, as it always was.

Forty years alone, but not much longer.

He didn't belong in this world anymore. Cars made of plastic. Smash one of those into the front end of a 1948 Packard Super Eight Deluxe or a 1950 Cadillac Coupe DeVille, and those big bumpers would shatter the plastic into bits. Engines so full of computers he knew he couldn't even change the oil. Talk of making electric cars; he could see them top-end of fifty-five, maybe. Put one of those motors in a pickup and it wouldn't be able to tow a fart in a whirlwind.

He used to drive out and look at the old farm, buildings all gone, but he saw them clearly, in a 1962 pickup that ran like it did when it was new, well, almost; old, but good enough for him.

They took it away from him after he hit that car in front of the post office. Hadn't even seen it. Took his license, too. Sold the snow blower; what good was it?

On the farm he'd listen to the CBC, *Hockey Night in Canada*, Foster Hewitt, greatest hockey broadcaster. Later he watched hockey on TV, but he'd already seen it through Hewitt's words. At the Menninger Café he tried to tell those young sprouts that given modern training and equipment the players of his day—Gordie Howe, the "Rocket," Jean Beliveau, "Boom Boom" Geoffrion, Bobby Hull, Ted Lindsay— would match up with Gretsky, Lemieux, Jagr, any of the newer heroes.

Dragged back in time, the modern goal scorers and defensemen would stand up well against the older group, but he didn't think the goalies would. He didn't think Roy, Brodeur, or Hasek, would be able to face Rocket Richard bearing down on them in the old Montreal Forum without their protective masks and helmets; not the way the great Terry Sawchuk, Harry Lumley, Jacques Plante, Glenn Hall, even old Gump Worsley faced flying pucks night after night, sometimes getting hit in the noggin. That quieted the scoffers.

Then his old TV went bad. Got a new one. Couldn't even turn it on. The neighbor boy did some things with the remote. Showed him the on-off button, the channel selector, the volume. Didn't understand it, but it worked. Smart kid.

Operations for cataracts, for glaucoma; not much good. He couldn't even see the TV screen. Sold the set. Nothing to watch anyway. Comedy shows with words that men used to get beaten up for using around someone's wife. Drama shows that had to be full of some weird allusions and pronouncements the coffee shop men called "political correctness." News shows that constantly put America down and villainized patriotism.

During the War, he and his wife would listen to the war news. So did their neighbors. Battle of the Bulge. V-E Day. Iwo Jima. Okinawa. V-J. Day. Americans were winning; the reporters were Americans, too. And talked like it. People loved America.

He sank heavily into his chair. Thought of the neighbor boy. Had to hire him to mow his grass, had his own rig; clean the snow from his walk, wintertime he turned his mower into a snow blower. Trimmed around the trees and house for no charge. Same with clearing snow off the back deck. Gone to college now.

Had to hire that scamp down the block; charged extra for trimming, extra for the back deck.

The room was dark; he struggled his way out of the chair and shuffled into the kitchen, the one room where he kept the shades up; it was her room. He put two slices in the toaster; poured Cheerios in a bowl; the same meal he'd had for breakfast, but it was enough. Grape jelly on the toast. Spilled the milk while pouring. Almost cursed, but caught himself.

Sarah hated cursing; he used to swear like a sailor who'd dropped a monkey wrench on his bare foot. Early in their marriage, he'd been in the barn, jammed his finger on something—he couldn't remember what—and let out with a stream of profanity that almost set the building on fire. He didn't know she had come in until she stood in front of him, her blue eyes sad, her face unsmiling. "Please, Eddie, I wish you wouldn't curse so; it offends God and it offends me."

He wasn't so sure God would be offended by anything he said, except if he took His Name in vain, but he felt lousy making Sarah feel bad. He apologized. It took him over a year, but he broke himself of that habit. Just for her.

Her beautiful eyes. He was sad that he'd never gotten the chance to take Sarah to Hawaii. Somewhere he'd read that the water in some of the bays turned a bright blue under the sky, and he would have liked to have seen if that blue even compared with her eyes. He doubted it.

He saw them walking in the sand, holding hands, a light wind stirring the palm fronds, the waves curling onto the beach. Maybe that was what Heaven was like.

He sat at the table and ate slowly; he had nothing else to do. His knotted fingers gnarled around the spoon. A doctor said, "Try this cream; it's supposed to work." He rubbed it into his fingers and hands; it didn't.

He rinsed the plate, the bowl, the knife, and the spoon and left them to dry. He walked to a cabinet and opened it, stared in; little brown bottles. Pills. Two kinds for his blood pressure, two kinds for his prostate problems, two diuretics, a blood thinner, one each for his a-fib, his diabetes, acid reflux, thyroid condition, cholesterol control. Vitamins and supplements to replace those the medications had leached out of his system.

Child-proof caps; he must have become a child for he couldn't get them open. He'd take a supplement bottle to the vise in the garage, tighten it in, and force the cap to release with a twist of a locking pliers. But then there'd be a seal which he couldn't raise with his fingernail: there was a thin plastic tab he was supposed to use, but usually it tore off before the seal released, so he'd jab the seal with a screwdriver and pry it off.

In the fridge were two bottles to control eye pressures. He hadn't used either of them in five days. The pills in their little brown bottles even longer.

He remembered his doctor telling him his urine was among the most expensive in town. He smiled.

Yesterday Shirley, the earnest young home-care nurse from County Health, had been there. She was concerned about him—his heart, among other things—and asked him about his medications. Was he neglecting to take them? No, he wasn't neglecting them; he showed her the bottles. Over the past six weeks he had not neglected them. He had taken out the daily requirement and flushed the pills down the toilet.

She told him just because he lived alone, he shouldn't let the housework go. He said he wouldn't. She said if she didn't see improvement in a month, he'd have to go to the clinic. He said that would be fine.

She had come once a week. Budget cuts. Then twice a month. Budget cuts. In a month the way his heart pounded at night; his heartburn; the pressure in his ears; his gasping for breath. In a month....

He did some dusting after she had gone. Tried vacuuming; quit, exhausted. He went out to feed the birds—the brown sparrows, like mice of the air; the greedy grackles; the outrageous blue jays; the mourning doves, not peaceful as doves were supposed to be, but always pecking at and chasing each other; a downy woodpecker; an occasional grosbeak; and his favorite, the chickadee, never greedy, flitting in to take one seed, then to the bushes, then back for another seed. Sometimes it would come to his hat. He liked the little bird.

Sarah liked the birds, the main reason he still fed them.

In a month...buttonholes that seemed to have gotten smaller through the years—at least he had more trouble pushing the buttons through them; cans that wouldn't stay on the can opener; packages of food he couldn't tear open, needed scissors; annoying phone calls.

He passed the time in the sunlight outdoors, in the brightness of the kitchen, in the twilight of the living room, lost in the darkness of the bedroom. He spoke to no one; read a little in the Large Print editions of Perry Mason novels; and waited.

He used to dream a lot. Some in color. Now just the one dream, dreary and dark. He was in a long, narrow boat on a ghost river. A thin sliver of light revealed a black figure in the prow that he knew was Death. The figure pulled the paddle through the water, raised it, transferred it to the other side of the boat, and pulled it through the water again. The paddle went back to the other side and the same rhythmic routine was repeated. And repeated, never varying.

There were no sounds, not even from the water dripping from the paddle. There were no smells from the shore, if the ghost river even had a shore.

He was heading somewhere.

In the morning he couldn't eat. He put on his hat, his coat, took the bird seed container and the peanuts; walked into the sunlight. Dark images fluttered across his sight. He filled the bird feeders and shuffled toward the house. A raucous jay flew in, grabbed a peanut, and flew off. The other birds waited.

Halfway to the house, the container fell from his hand. He groaned and followed it.

After the man lay silent and unmoving for a few minutes, the birds flew in. Chirping, croaking, chattering, eating. On the feeders; on the ground.

The little chickadee left the lilac bush and flew to the man's hat, still strangely on his head. She searched, but found nothing and flew back to the lilac, waiting for a chance among the larger birds. There would be something left for her.

The sun moved on. The old man was well on his way to wherever he was going.

A LOVE STORY

Oil was under his fingernails, around his fingernails, in the creases and grooves of his hands. His clothes smelled of oil; his work vehicle reeked of it. Western North Dakota was awash in oil. Under the ground, above ground in the tanks, moving in the trucks, rail cars, and pipelines. Oil lubricated the economy. Oil was money. Money for merchants, business people, clerks, custodians, and cocktail waitresses. Money for him.

Then the world was awash in oil and the bottom fell out.

He'd worked his way up from "worm" on the rig floor where he tackled the big wrenches called tongs and the tugger winch, to chain hand before automation took that job, to motorman because of his aptitude for motors and pumps, and always dreamed of moving up—derrickman and even the kingpin, toolpusher, who was responsible for all the crews and usually was not contaminated with oil.

As prices dropped, men were laid off. He looked ahead and handed in his time. His boss talked with him, wished him well, and said he had a job if things turned around.

He left his man-camp in Big Muddy with no regrets, threw his gear into the back of the Ford F-150 he'd purchased for a shade under thirty thousand, and headed east on the Red Highway. He'd rarely had time to drive the pickup and it still smelled new after two years. The traffic, especially the trucks, had fallen from a bedlam of congestion to almost normal for western North Dakota.

He checked into the Grand International Hotel on North Hill in

Minot and enjoyed the hottest shower and the best night's rest he'd had in four years. He stayed in bed and studied his hands, wondering if they'd ever be clean. He thought about how much money he'd made in just four years, more than some men made in half a lifetime, and smiled. He remembered the farm on which he'd grown up, just outside of Fishtown.

He went down for breakfast; over-tipped the smiling, efficient waitress; and headed back south through the traffic and onto the Red Highway, then split off onto the Northwest Highway.

A couple hours of driving and he passed Fishtown, kept going a few miles and pulled off. His farm was there; rented out; his folks living in the Twin Cities, close to his sister and her family. The machine shed was in good shape, green tractor standing guard, but the house and the barn had been made derelict by wind and rain in just ten years. Neither he nor his brother wanted to farm, so his Dad rented the land and pulled out. Harsh words, bad feelings, his Dad feeling betrayed.

He felt ashamed he hadn't seen his folks in over four years, thinking that texting was good enough. Even longer for his older brother, an insurance salesman in Fresno, California.

He looked across a field and was surprised by the emptiness south of a grove. He'd spent many hours in the yard playing ball and in the now-gone house with his two cousins. As he watched, wind juddered the weeds which showed along the old foundations.

His uncle had been in Vietnam and came home whole. When he was fourteen, he asked him about the fighting there. His uncle said, "The war taught me it's better to kill than be killed," and never spoke about it again.

In Fishtown he saw one of his old high school buddies, who was a bartender. They shot buckets and played Horse in his driveway, had an early dinner together before his friend had to open the bar, then he went wandering around the town. The clash between what Fishtown had been and what it had become depressed him.

He stopped at the school, reported to the office as per the notice, and a secretary escorted him around the halls he and his jock friends used to rule. He wasn't allowed to go any place without her. She was nice, but had other things to do. Before he left, he asked her about his old teachers. There were none left—retired, moved on, or dead. At least the names she recognized.

When he asked her about Miss Genevieve Powers, she did know her. She was in the nursing home over in Menninger.

He and his buddy had supper together with two of their FHS classmates, both divorced, and he stayed over in the second bedroom; the women seemed willing; he wasn't. The bed was lumpy, and he regretted his decision not to stay in the tiny motel—it's bed couldn't have been worse.

In the morning his body felt awful: the mattress and the basketball aggravated muscles oil field work hadn't strengthened. His friend had a hangover, so he thanked him for the hospitality and drove to the café. After breakfast, he gassed up at the Amalgamated Farmers' station, four cents a gallon more than in Big Muddy.

Waiting for the tank to fill, he studied his shadow-streaked fingers. He checked his mileage: not as good as he had hoped. He took the West Highway, flipped on his sunglasses, and drove into the early morning glare.

There was an Alabama girl in Fort Stockton when he was helping maintain some of the over three hundred productive wells in the Yates Oil Field, bringing up Texas petroleum from the Permian Basin. Fun-loving, not too serious about anything but money, the prettiest barmaid in the entire cowboy-oil worker bar, he fell for her forever, he thought. They soon discovered they were good for each other in bed. He couldn't get her out of his mind.

Big romantic evening, red rose on the table, champagne and lobster, the works. After the meal and some champagne, he got down on his knee, she smiled, he proposed, she laughed. "Ya'll think ah'm gonna marry ah boy with oily han's. A doctor or lawyer, maybe. Quit funnin' an' le's go ta bed."

His whole world turned red. He cursed, threw the ring; it bounced off the table, and he was gone. Her boisterous laugh chased him out the door.

He packed up and headed for North Dakota.

Twenty minutes later he turned off and drove north, past a row of tall evergreens that were a lot smaller when the FHS bus brought the basketball team to Menninger, and he would get all excited, seeing the trees and knowing he was a starter.

He knew the town a little—he'd dated a couple girls there—and turned onto Lamborn. At the nursing home desk, he asked to speak with Miss Powers. He explained who he was.

The receptionist's face brightened. "Oh, how nice, Genevieve will be so glad to see you. I think they're all in the solarium; they like to go there after breakfast and enjoy the sun. She's wide awake mentally, but her stroke made it difficult for her to speak."

They passed through a door and into a bright room filled with people in wheelchairs or sitting at small tables. Eyes, expectant or hesitant, looked at him, then looked away. "Someone to see you, Genevieve."

A shrunken woman looked up from her wheelchair. Except for her eyes he wouldn't have recognized her, but he would never forget those kind brown eyes belonging to the teacher who had taken an interest in a devil-may-care kid and pushed, pulled, and struggled to get him to graduate.

"Here's a chair; I have to get back. Enjoy your visit."

He thanked her and sat down. At first he didn't think she knew him, but when he began talking and expressing his thanks, she reached out and caressed his cheek. He took one of her hands in his and she clasped her other hand on top. He kept talking as he looked around; maybe touching was against the rules.

When he looked at her again, big tears were scuttling down her cheeks, momentarily diverted by her wrinkles. Her mouth was moving, but there was no sound. It was an agony. He couldn't stay.

He said he had to leave and stood up. Her eyes were pleading…for what? He left the room, thanked the receptionist, and went outside.

There were many residents and visitors on the large cement patio, enjoying the spring sun. Some were walking slowly or using walkers;

others were sitting in chairs or wheelchairs. Some were talking; other just sat in the sunshine.

He had to sit down; he could feel the tears, turned toward the building, and wiped his eyes. There was an empty chair beside an older man dressed in black, wearing a clerical collar. He was intent on a small book with a black cover.

"Mind if I sit down?"

The man looked up. "No, no, not at all. It's a glorious morning."

He sat. An elderly man pushed a wheelchair onto the patio. As it went by, he saw the occupant was a gray-haired woman with a misshapen head, protected by headgear and between two headrests. The man stopped, made certain the sun was on her, but not in her eyes, and pulled a chair beside her.

"Now that is a real love story."

"What?"

The man in black pointed toward the wheelchair. "Are you from around here?"

"Fishtown, originally." He was trying to hide his hands; the older man's hands were immaculately white, his fingernails clean and well-kept. They closed on the New Testament.

"You in a hurry?"

"Not really."

"Heading somewhere?"

"Not really."

"Got time for a story…about them." He nodded at the wheelchair.

"Sure."

"Her name is Donna. Her family came here when her Dad was hired as a pharmacist. Her mother got a job in a dress shop on Chicago Street. She started seventh grade here. You've heard of sparkling personalities; Donna's was sparkling plus. She wasn't the prettiest girl in the class, but she became the most well-liked. In the Senior Poll she was voted the Friendliest, and that was by the kids in grades nine to eleven. When I took over my church here, I looked up some of her classmates—there are still some around—including her best friend,

Barbara, and every one of them commented on her personality, but none of them could really define it or pin it down.

"Up on Villard over there (he pointed at the street a block south) in the business district is the Waterman Auditorium. Every Saturday night there was roller skating. Sometimes on Friday nights there would be dances or parties for the kids the community would host.

"It soon became apparent, especially at roller skating, that three young boys were more interested in Donna than their peers were. One of them was George, the man with her now. Jackson and Frankie were the other two.

"All three of them were excellent skaters and so was Donna. On couples' skates, she was always with one of them; she didn't play favorites, much to their chagrin. Some skaters would just stand and watch her and whichever one she was with. It didn't matter; it was always graceful and rhythmical in time with the music.

"At dances, too, it was always the Three plus One.

"Donna couldn't date until she was fourteen and then just to go a movie at the Blackstone, the local theatre, or bowling at Amazon Lanes. When she did, it was always with one of the three.

"However, by the time she could go out of town on dates, George was slowly falling behind. In the Senior Poll he was voted as the Boy with the Best Manners. He was considerate, probably the nicest of the three, the smallest—you saw him go by—an average student. I'm not saying why he was edged out; only Donna knew. His parents were members of my congregation before they came here to the Home, and I talked with them many times, but they had no idea why George was always third. They did love him very much, even after he stopped going to church. Now they're in the cemetery north of town. I can't talk to George; he won't speak to me.

"Frankie was the wild one. Black leather jacket, Harley, juvenile troubles with the law, devil-take-the-hindmost student, drank some. I guess he came by that naturally: his Dad was a bartender and his Mom was a barmaid. His name never showed up in the Senior Poll

"Jackson was the intellectual or thought he was. An honor student; football, basketball, baseball player. Had the most money.

Voted Most Likely to Succeed in the Senior Poll. His father ran an insurance and real estate agency on Villard; his mother did all kinds of charity work and fundraisers in the community. They lived up on the Hill (he gestured to the east where the town went into an incline), which was the exclusive neighborhood, although it's not as exclusive as it once was. You had to have money and social prestige to live there then; now just about anyone can. I have a home there so that shows you what I mean."

He was looking at his hands, wondering, *Would enough Go-Jo get out the grime?*

"By their junior year, George was outside looking in, but Jackson and Frankie were like two bulls facing off. They had never liked each other, and it was agony for one of them when his rival was on a date with Donna.

"It came to a head at prom time. Both of them asked her, and she couldn't make up her mind. Finally, for whatever reason—Barbara told me Donna never confided that to her—she chose Jackson. He did the Victory Strut around school, especially in front of Frankie. He was lucky Frankie didn't tear his head off; he had huge biceps and a short fuse. Jackson's parents went all out on the tux, the flowers, and the limo to take Donna and Jackson and six of their friends to the Chuck Wagon in Sacred Water after the prom. They'd rented the place and paid the staff to stay and serve the meal.

"It was a glorious night; Donna even let Jackson kiss her several times.

"For Frankie it was a night of torment. He got some booze, jumped on his cycle, and drank himself silly out in the country. Missed the curve leading to the overpass south of town. Broke his ankle. Ended up in the ditch where no one found him until daylight. The kids who went to see him in the hospital said his one leg, side, and arm were all gauzed up, and when the wounds healed, he was only too glad to show them the dark raspberries crusting his flesh. He felt like a hero because Donna believed she was responsible and turned more attention to him and away from Jackson.

"She helped Frankie study for his Finals and he barely scraped through, much to Jackson's disgust. All that summer it was Donna and Frankie, who was on crutches and then limping along. Soon Jackson saw he was limping a lot more when Donna was around. He tried to tell Donna, but she wouldn't believe him. That made him even more angry.

"Their senior year Jackson eased his way back in and by prom time it was fifty-fifty on dates with Donna. But she chose Frankie for the prom. Jackson took a girl from Caseyville, got her some punch, and left her alone while he cut in on Frankie as much as possible. His date cried all the way back to Caseyville."

I wonder if Lava Soap would do the trick or something else with pumice. He put his hands in his lap again.

"Frankie had a job on a farm northwest of town during the summer. Ankle as strong as ever. Jackson was a lifeguard again, just for the sun, and worked it around his Legion baseball schedule. They had alternate weekend dates with Donna. She told Barbara she liked them both, but didn't like their constant attempts to go beyond second base.

"Jackson left for the University in Grand Forks that fall; Frankie kept up with the farm work until after harvest. Donna had gotten a part-time job as a clerk in the drug store, where her Dad worked. The customers liked her friendliness and her smile, and so did the owner.

"What he didn't like was Frankie hanging around every time Donna worked, so he told her that either Frankie had to stay away or she'd lose her job: the customers didn't like having a juvenile delinquent and biker monopolizing Donna's time when they needed her help. She told Frankie; he stopped coming.

"Jackson tried to get home as often as possible; he didn't want Frankie to have a clear field. In the fall Donna would date Frankie on one Saturday night and Jackson on the next one. During the winter when Jackson was stuck in Grand Forks a lot, Frankie took her out three of every four Saturdays. He even got her to drink a little beer, but she refused to give up her virtue.

"Jackson didn't make the baseball team, so he had a full spring to share Donna. Then it was summer. When he discovered she liked a beer or two, he began bringing beer: two for her and four for him. He'd learned something at UND.

"Just before it was time for the colleges to reopen, their old high school classmates organized a party in an abandoned farmstead, complete with a keg, a pony keg, some six-packs, and a bonfire with wood from the old outhouse and a shed. The flames attracted attention; the sheriff's department was called. When someone saw the cop cars approaching, everyone fired out of the yard and headed in the other three directions. The county men knew what had been going on, but did not pursue because they didn't want to provoke any accidents, fatal or otherwise. They extinguished the fire and left.

"Donna had her first car, a 1962 Ford Falcon and had persuaded Jackson and Frankie to ride with her to the party. All three of them filled up at the keg too often, and when the alarm came, barely made it to the Falcon. Donna was clearly in no shape to drive, so Jackson slid in, started the engine, and followed two dim taillights in the dusty cloud ahead of him on the gravel road. As they passed section roads, more and more cars pulled off and finally Jackson took one and drove west, across the Gold Star Highway and kept going.

"They could see the lights of Menninger far off to the south. He kept going west as they laughed and relived their narrow escape. Frankie had even hooked three beers on the run and they popped and drank them.

"Jackson turned south and a few miles later went east on a road where the county maintainer had made a windrow of gravel. Donna checked her watch and said she had to get home; she was already too late. Jackson pushed the accelerator. The little car started fishtailing back and forth, but he kept it under control. Frankie said to let it out or he'd take over and show Jackson how. Faster, then faster. A front wheel caught the windrow; there was no saving it; they went off the shoulder and into the ditch, the Falcon rolling crazily.

"All three were thrown out. Jackson and Frankie were clear; Donna was pinned under the chassis. When Jackson and Frankie regained consciousness, they heard her moaning."

He had been ready to excuse himself, but any kind of accident interested him; he decided to hear the rest of the story.

"They were all bleeding, but Donna was the worst. They couldn't budge the car. The farm Frankie worked on was a quarter mile away; he went to get a tractor. Jackson reached under the car and held Donna's hand. He said everything would be all right; she said she knew it would be. It was just her legs, so cold she couldn't feel them. They said the Lord's Prayer. Frankie finally arrived; he was so drunk he couldn't start the tractor at first, then drove slowly to avoid hitting the ditch.

"He drove into the ditch and stopped in front of the wreck. Jackson got up to help him; Donna's blood dripped off his hand. Frankie got the front-end loader in position, and he and Jackson wound a chain around it. Jackson couldn't see where to attach it to the chassis, so Frankie got a flashlight from the tool kit, and they crawled around, looking. Finally, they just hooked it around the axle.

"Frankie weaved his way to the seat; Jackson told Donna not to cry, she'd soon be free. Frankie moved the lever, the loader started upward, so did the Falcon. Then it moved sideways and down; the chain had slipped along the axle. Donna screamed, a brief finality. The Falcon was on her head.

"The farmer, thinking someone had stolen his tractor, pulled up. A flashlight guided him into the ditch. After he saw what had happened, he secured the chain, told the 'young fools' to get clear, and raised the car.

"Looking at the mess that was Donna's head, he didn't know if he should call the ambulance or the coroner. He threw his jacket over her, told the two boys not to touch her, and raced home.

"Donna was taken to the hospital in Kingston, but they could do nothing; then to Fargo, where they stabilized her. She spent three months undergoing surgeries, surviving in intensive care.

"The boys faced a gauntlet of charges. Jackson had one of the best attorneys in the state; Frankie's lawyer passed the Bar exam on his second try and then just barely. Jackson had to pay fines and costs; his jail time was suspended. Frankie was found guilty of reckless endangerment or some such charge, couldn't afford to pay much, and served six months in jail.

"His parents were not members of my congregation. In fact, they had no church; neither did Frankie. They lost their jobs to alcohol and to the grief they felt about their son's part in the accident and anger over his treatment, compared to Jackson. They were here in the Home and I talked with them when I made my regular rounds.

"Almost as soon as Frankie got out, he was drafted and sent to Vietnam, where everyone could see the Communists were going to win eventually, so keep your head down and don't be a hero.

"He came home to Menninger, saw Donna once, and left the next day on his old cycle which had been in storage. His folks never saw nor heard from him again. A few years later his motorcycle was found at the bottom of a cliff off the Pacific Coast Highway, his body presumably washed out to sea.

"Jackson went back to school, but rarely visited his folks, rarely came to Menninger. There was a lot of resentment in the community against him, and it spilled over onto his family. His father's business fell off, his mother was invited to fewer and fewer parties and was no longer welcome on fundraisers. After Jackson graduated, they sold the business and their house and moved to Los Angeles.

"Jackson was lost. He joined a Pentecostal church, took some medical classes, and joined a group of medical missionaries in Central America. They stayed in a large village and made week-long treks to smaller villages, where they would work on water systems and do what healing they could. He even found a girl, Alejandra, he started to like. But he wanted to go slowly and not rush into anything.

"When he was gone on a trek, government troops came into the village. They had been chasing some rebels, who had confiscated supplies from the villagers. The captain accused the village of being a bunch of traitors. A village elder spoke up and denied the accusation. A rifle butt silenced him. Six villagers were chosen at random and executed. The soldiers moved out: no help to the rebels or we'll be back.

"When the missionaries returned, it took several weeks for

the villagers to associate with them: the government might see the missionaries as sympathetic to the rebel side. Jackson spent a lot of time with Alejandra. She trusted him when he said if the villagers just raised and harvested their crops and paid their taxes, the soldiers would leave them alone.

"Two months later there was another trek, even farther into the jungle. Alejandra kissed him goodbye. A few days later some rebels entered the village. They said the villagers were collaborating with the government and giving the soldiers information about the rebels' whereabouts. They claimed that was how the government troops had been able to set an ambush two days before and kill six of them. The village headman tried to explain they hadn't even seen any soldiers for a couple months. The rebel leader shot him in the mouth. They chose six people at random—four men and two women—and shot them in the back of the head. Alejandra was one of them.

"After that, Jackson just wanted out.

"Back in the States he joined a commune near Taos, New Mexico, devoted to protecting the environment through organic farming, equality in sharing, and peace. The commune failed because everyone wanted to talk about growing crops, but no one really devoted much time to it. It was just too hard.

"He wandered off into the Rockies; the winter drove him out. He tried the California drug culture, but the smoking, pill popping, and acid trips just made him sick or empty. He walked up a mountain outside of L.A. and lived in a solar worshipping commune. An old L.A. millionaire would drive up a couple times a month and give cash to the leader, known as Sol's Voice. Sol and his band of Sun Guards would drive a rickety pickup into the city, get supplies, and bring them back. Chastity was the rule and was preached as the Sun God's ideal. It wasn't a strong selling point for the males—females outnumbered them five to one—so to help solidify his rule, Sol's Voice offered positions in the Sun Guards to promising males to replace those who left for one reason or another. He told Jackson that when they made their supply runs, they always stopped at a fashionable whorehouse.

The next day Jackson went down the mountain; he couldn't stand the hypocrisy.

"He ended up at Big Sur, overlooking the Pacific, sitting on a mountain, staring at the persistent pounding of the waves against the dark rocks. His constant companion, black guilt, sat beside him... Do you know 'General William Booth Enters Into Heaven' by Vachel Lindsay?"

He remembered his high school English class. "Yes, we read it in Miss Powers' class. She even had kids playing the instruments, bass drum, flute, tambourines."

"I should have guessed that...Miss Powers. Well, Jackson was rolling his high school days through his mind when he thought of his old English teacher, cut from the same cloth as Miss Powers, I imagine. The same poem; the same instruments playing, but also a banjo player. He saw Donna playing the flute. Then the refrain started pounding in his head: 'Are you washed in the blood of the Lamb?' He lay back and stared at the sky: 'Are you washed in the blood of the Lamb?'

"Then he recalled from the Bible: 'Though your sins be as scarlet, they shall be white as snow.' He walked down the mountain and hitched his way to L.A. on the Pacific Coast Highway. The first church he came to, he went in, prayed, and recommitted his life to Christ. His acceptance of Jesus when his Bible School teacher had asked for such acceptance was more due to peer pressure than understanding on his part.

"Jackson was lucky. He was able to reconcile with his folks after years of separation. His Dad died three months later. His Mom still had some friends in Menninger with whom she corresponded. She wrote to them a lot of the things I've told you. When I took the church here, many of them were still alive, even though most were here in the Home. Some of them had forgiven Jackson; some still hated his insides.

"For his part, Jackson went back to school, got a couple degrees, and went about preaching the joy of forgiveness. After his mother died, he moved up and down the Coast, living in several cities, the guilt washed away."

George stood up and turned the wheelchair. It went by, George looking straight ahead. He tried to imagine the twisted little woman as a cheerleader or playing the flute, but couldn't. The automatic door opened and the couple went inside.

"As for George; well, you've seen him the way he's been for almost fifty years. He owns and manages the C-Store up on the Gold Star, but he is down here every day to be with Donna. Unless the flu or some "bug" halts visitation or if he's sick, I don't think he's missed a half dozen days, and that was because of blizzards. As I said, a love story."

The men were silent for awhile. He stared at his hands; they didn't look so grimy. Then he said, "I should be going. Thanks for the story, Father. I was glad to listen."

"My pleasure. Found some place to go to?"

"Yeah, I think I'll head for the Twin Cities and then maybe out to California. Got some people to see." He stood. "By the way, my name is Ross; Kent Ross."

The man in black stood and put out his hand. "Glad to know you, Kent, but I'm not a Catholic priest. I'm the Lutheran pastor and part-time chaplain at the Home here. I'm Rev. Ellingson...Jackson Ellingson."

A SAGA

The doughty young prince gazed up at the flinty mountain. Proud was he. Conqueror of the storm-tossed waves. Crosser of the Great Reg Desert, trackless, waterless. Now only the mountain remained.

The young champion began the climb. The rocks were sharp; the wind was fierce. Many times he fell, but would not be dismayed. He arose and with his strong will, endured the end of his journey.

Before the cave of the witch, horrible to behold, he called forth. When she appeared, he averted his eyes, lest she prove Medusa.

Her cackling voice bade him enter. Standing in the coldness of the cavern, she asked him his purpose.

"To gaze into the Mirror of All-Knowledge."

"And what is your forfeit, Sir Knight?"

"All I possess."

"Cast away your war trappings."

His sword, shield, and crested helm rang on the flinty floor.

She beckoned. Her hideous laughter and vile stench led him to a narrow grotto. A light, mysterious. He sat on a stone, cold and unyielding. The witch, horrible to behold, drew a black shroud and, there, the Mirror.

She spoke. She told him he would be without food or wine, that he may grow cold, but that he would witness the wonders of the world.

She gave the Shield of Faith to his hand, set the Helmet of Hope

185

on his youthful head, and placed the Sword of Despair by his side, then withdrew, a cunning hag.

The young warrior beheld the Mirror. It revealed the order of the universe, creation, destruction, stars, planets, the Earth. The day ended; the questing prince smiled and slept.

The morning brought forth rendings and retchings of continents; volcanoes, spewing; mountains growing and dying. Blood coursed through the young heart.

The new morning came. With it, Life. Tiny, barely seen. Then things roiling in the waters; crawling things etching the land; flourishing in the air. Monsters, huge and unknown; dragons of bulk or danger. Filled with wonder was the warrior.

The next morning. The wily witch spied on him. Wonderful life passed in the mirror. Grass, flowers, trees. The youthful knight smiled at the bounty. Then animals, familiar and unfamiliar. The changes each kind underwent as eons passed. The dying out; the coming again; the renewal of life. Joy was in his heart. The ancient crone nodded knowingly.

The last morning brought humans. The Knight-Errant watched their appearance, growth, development. The activities, foreign to other beings. Their achievements; their violence. Not in a knightly fashion. The tortured existence of the weak. The screams of women, the cries of children, the destruction of life in wars and ways unimagined. Colder than the rock was his body. Then the mirror revealed the future.

That evening the knowing old witch, horrible to behold, entered the grotto. The Shield of Faith had been tossed aside. The Helmet of Hope had been dashed on the rocky floor. The princeling was cold; he had thrust the Sword of Despair through his heart.

Printed in the United States
By Bookmasters